ADDICTED TO ANSLEY

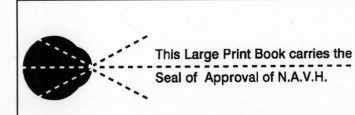

This Large Print Book carries the
Seal of Approval of N.A.V.H.

ADDICTED TO ANSLEY

LINDA KAGE

THORNDIKE PRESS
A part of Gale, Cengage Learning

GALE
CENGAGE Learning·

Detroit • New York • San Francisco • New Haven, Conn • Waterville, Maine • London

GALE
CENGAGE Learning®

LIBRARY OF CONGRESS CATALOGING-IN-PUBLICATION DATA

Kage, Linda.
    Addicted to Ansley / By Linda Kage. — Large Print edition.
    pages cm. — (Thorndike Press Large Print Clean Reads.)
    ISBN 978-1-4104-6332-6 (hardcover) — ISBN 1-4104-6332-X (hardcover)
    1. Family secrets—Fiction. 2. Fathers and daughters—Fiction. 3. Large type books. I. Title.
    PS3611.A34A65 2013
    813'.6—dc23   2013032226

Published in 2013 by arrangement with Black Lyon Publishing, LLC

Printed in the United States of America
1 2 3 4 5 6 7 17 16 15 14 13

For the Martinies:
Mike, Sandra, Adam, Alaina,
and Matthew.
And for Shi Ann, too.
Thank you for entertaining Lydia and me
on those long, lonely nights we were
home alone.

CHAPTER ONE

As a motivational speaker, Ward Gemmell decided he totally rocked.

Every behind in J. Edgar Hoover High School sat planted on the edge of the bleacher seats in their gymnasium as each student leaned forward, captivated by him. Him of all people. It flattered, thrilled, yet downright terrified him. And all he'd had to do to create such a buzz was stand before them, open a vein, and let the biggest mistakes of his life bleed out of his mouth.

No problem.

He could own up. Mostly.

Still, even as he managed to keep his voice smooth and even, his freezing hands trembled uncontrollably inside his pockets where he kept them securely stuffed.

"I know what it's like," he insisted into the microphone, unnerved when his own voice boomed throughout the enormous arena. "I was your age. I walked the halls of a high school exactly like this one. And I became addicted to drugs."

He'd been speaking to them for about twenty-five minutes now, the slight rasp in his voice testimony to his lengthy monologue. But regardless of the ticking clock, all ears remained tuned in with fixated absorption.

"I know how easy it is to fall victim to the lure, how fun the wild nights seem . . . for a while. And I know how much it hurts when you realize you've destroyed yourself. But most importantly, I know how hard it is to break free. Yet I'm standing here today, to tell you, you can. And once you get control of your own life again, it will be the best thing you ever did."

He paused to wipe a cold, damp film of sweat covering his palms against the interior of his pockets as he glanced at the young, avid faces surrounding him. "And I'm also here to tell you you'll need help on this journey. I tried a dozen times to make a go of it on my own only to end up getting even more dependent. It wasn't until I sought a center exactly like Danny's Haven that I was able to take the initial step in the right direction. Yes, you'll still bust your —"

He broke off abruptly to cringe as the silence of his near expletive echoed through the speaker system. Half the audience laughed before he leaned forward to apologize.

"Sorry about that. I meant . . . you'll do the work — plenty of work — but people will be with you the whole way, every step, striving to help you just as hard as you strive to help yourself. That's the key to detoxing. No one can help you unless you're serious about quitting. And at Danny's Haven, we're committed to you. If you're in it for the long haul, then so are we. No one has to break their addiction alone. You can receive help. And with us, you will. Thank you."

With a gracious nod, he stepped back and ducked his head slightly when the clapping started. It rattled him every time he received an applause after he detailed exactly how messed up he'd been. Oh, you did drugs? Here's a hearty slap on the back. Congratulations.

Wasn't like he'd discovered the cure for cancer or saved a hundred lives in one heroic act. He'd just broken free from a nasty lifestyle. Yet they continued to clap.

It boggled his mind.

He released one hand from his pockets to run shaky fingers through his mahogany hair and offered the students a tense, grateful smile along with an appreciated half-wave before backing up five paces and sinking gratefully into the cold metal chair beside the podium. Next to him, Care stood and concluded the presentation, telling the student body how they could contact Danny's Haven and get information.

Desi had no doubt already set up the booth in the lobby, full of pamphlets and flyers to pass out. He wished he could switch places with her, at least once. He'd happily set up the booth. But Desi, like many of the other counselors at Danny's Haven, had never done drugs. She couldn't give a personalized account the way he could. Ward folded his hands in his lap and concentrated on keeping his back straight because he was a habitual sloucher. He hoped he looked professional and polished, because inside, he felt raw and battle scarred, exactly how his speeches always left him. Torn open, exposed, and worthless.

It had never stopped him from standing in front of hundreds of teens at a time, however. If his words induced one kid to clean up his act, then he considered all the anguish worth it.

But seriously, the constant reminder of what he used to be definitely knew how to keep a guy humble.

This had to be the twentieth — or possibly the hundredth — presentation Danny's Haven had given in the seven years since he'd been hired on to the team, and it continued to leave him rattled afterward. He suspected Care understood the shredded nerves he had because just as she did after every testimony he gave, she set her hand on his shoulder as she passed him and patted twice in her maternal way.

Shuddering out a steadying breath, he glanced up. She nodded and flickered him an approving smile — which was all he needed — before striding down the steps and off the makeshift stage. He stood and trailed her past the mass of seated students. When they pushed into the lobby, he breathed easier until he spotted Desi waiting nearby, wringing her hands and looking ready to burst into tears.

She rushed to Care, blurting, "I left the box of free pencils at the center."

Ward winced. The free pencils were their most popular promotional item. Everyone took a free pencil. But never one to flinch under pressure, Care merely lifted an unconcerned hand. "Doesn't matter. After Ward's speech in there, no one in that gymnasium will need a complimentary pencil to remember Danny's Haven."

Shoulders sagging with relief, Desi glanced toward him and winked. "Knock it out of the ballpark again, did ya, slugger?"

His smile held all the confidence he didn't feel. "As always."

"Way to go, bud." She held up her balled hand for him to fist bump. He obliged her and even bounced his shoulder against hers as she liked to do. Nevertheless, throughout their celebrating, his nerves remained strung taut. He already knew he wouldn't be able to relax until he was far and gone away from J. Edgar Hoover High and the space of hours separated them.

Inside the gym, he heard the principal take the microphone and wrap up their presentation, letting the students know they could stop by Desi's booth to pick up more information about Danny's Haven if they were interested. Then he dismissed classes for the day.

Seconds later, the flood began.

The double doors flew open, letting the crowd exit. Hundreds glanced their way, shifting their attention from Ward, to Care, and then to their table full of goodies. Only about a dozen teens moved toward them to glance over the brochures and flyers. Half of that number actually reached out and snagged a pamphlet.

Care, with her usual grace and charm, started a conversation with one boy loitering nearby, and Ward tried not to look uncomfortable. He wasn't sure which part of a school visit he hated more: getting up and spilling his guts to the mass of probing young eyes or starting a one-on-one exchange with them afterward. He sucked at opening a rapport with strangers.

"Nice job, Gemmell," a male voice caught his attention, causing Ward to swing right and nod at the approaching adult. Probably a teacher. "I had a nephew who got caught up in drugs." The man shook his head. "I forgot how many times he was busted. Ended up dying in jail."

"I'm sorry to hear that." Ward's chest tightened as he swallowed a lump in this throat. He heard similar tragic tales at every school assembly and wondered why he never improved at offering sympathy. "Jail isn't a pretty place to die."

And he would know. He'd spent a couple visits there himself.

The adult, who Ward soon learned was a math teacher, continued to chat his ear off. From the corner of his eyes, he saw a couple of teens lingering close by but not approaching. He silently sighed when a girl a dozen feet away who'd been fiddling with a scarf she wore as she shifted uneasily about turned and wandered off.

It always seemed to happen that way. Ward knew he couldn't help every troubled teen, but knowing a possible lost soul was escaping bothered him.

Twenty minutes later, the teacher had gone and their booth stood deserted. With quiet, economic efficiency, Ward, Care, and Desi worked together, packing up the leftover pamphlets, stowing them in boxes, and lugging them to the van.

"I'll go back for the folding table," he offered, dusting his hands onto his thighs. A November breeze ruffled his hair, making him shudder and tug the collar of his jacket up higher.

Care nodded. "Thanks. I think I'll head back to the center. See you there."

"I'll ride with you," Desi called after Care, hurrying to catch up.

As the two women climbed into Care's car, Ward waved them goodbye and returned to the gym for their table. He stalled a moment, warming his chilled hands by rubbing them together and blowing on them before he tipped the table onto its side and folded the legs. He heaved the heavy thing outside and made it halfway across the lawn, nearly to the Danny's Haven van, before a call stalled him.

"Excuse me? Mr. Gemmell?"

He glanced up. The girl he'd seen earlier dawdling near their booth waved at him. He could tell it was she from the multi-colored scarf draped over her shoulders. As he paused, allowing her to intercept him, she broke into a jog, her dark hair and scarf flowing out behind her. Setting the heavy table down and letting the side rest against his leg, he grinned at the wholesome-looking child.

"It's just Ward," he said. "The word mister makes me uncomfortable around the collar, like I should be wearing a tie or something."

When he gave a dreaded shiver for effect, she laughed. He froze when she brushed a piece of her long, dark hair behind her ear. A stunning girl, she looked pristine perfect up close like this. Too perfect to be seeking out a jaded Ward Gemmell.

Ward squinted, curious about what she needed. From the clean cut look of her — clear skin, white teeth, lucid blue eyes, and nothing else to denote a drug habit — he doubted she'd even know what a narcotic was if someone handed it to her and told her how to smoke it. It was possible she was associated with someone else getting in-volved and wanted Ward to intercede. In which case, he gladly would. But even that scenario didn't ring true. She didn't seem like the type to befriend an addict either.

Maybe she was a journalism student and wanted to interview him for an article in her school paper. He ground his teeth, hoping he could come up with some excuse to talk his way out of that. Only important people were interviewed.

Important he was not.

Or maybe —

Geez, maybe he should stop guessing and ask her outright. "What can I do for you?"

She sucked in a deep breath, drawing so much air into her lungs her chest heaved and her shoulders lifted briefly. Whatever she wanted to request, he could tell it was a monumental deal for her. Not sure what he could offer that could be so vital, he focused on her a little more sharply, leaning in just a tad closer.

"I want to volunteer," she finally exploded out her wish on a breathless exhale before quickly adding, "At Danny's Haven."

Ward pulled back, thinking no way he'd heard that right. "Volunteer?"

She bit her bottom lip and nodded. Something familiar about that move made him focus on her mouth. Blinking again, he studied the rest of her face, rattled by the unexplainable recognition inside him, something deep in his gut telling him he should know her.

He laughed uneasily. "Uh . . ." He glanced at the Danny's Haven van he'd driven here. The back double doors hung open, waiting for him to slide the folding table into the cargo space. But Care's car, which had been sitting next to it, had vanished. "Umm . . ." He turned back to the girl. "What's your name?"

She smiled, looking encouraged. "Brooklyn."

He sifted his hand through his hair. "I'm sorry, Brooklyn, but I'm not the best person to ask about this. My supervisor handles hiring volunteers. I don't set up this kind of thing, and . . . honestly, Danny's Haven isn't the safest place for a young lady to offer her time —"

"I don't mind," she cut in eagerly — too eagerly. "Really."

When he opened his mouth to gainsay her, she grabbed his arm.

He gaped at her slim fingers. They gripped his sleeve so tightly, so earnestly. Lifting his face, he was even more startled to find a desperate expression on her face. The sunlight caught glittering sparkles in her blue eyes as if gathering tears were preparing to dribble down her cheeks any second.

"Please," she whispered. "I never knew my dad. Mom says he was too addicted to drugs to be a part of my life. So I just . . . I can't help but think if I could work at your center, in any capacity, I'd feel like maybe I had helped him."

Mouth dropping open, Ward managed to choke out the word, "Wow." But seriously. How amazing could one girl get? He coughed violently into his fist. Needing to look away from this remarkable, compassionate child before he started bawling a little himself, he focused on the folded table digging into his thigh. After breathing in through his nose to settle his unruly feelings, he exhaled slowly.

"Okay," he rasped. "Wow. That's really . . . amazing actually. But yeah. Wow. Uh . . . you do realize it's a center for teens, right? And your father would no longer —"

"I know," she cut in with a wince. "But if I could volunteer at Danny's Haven, and maybe pay it forward, I wouldn't, I don't know . . . maybe I wouldn't feel so empty inside where he's concerned. Maybe I could convince myself he's clean and okay now because I helped someone like him."

Ward cleared his throat, still unable to look at her. Her tale hit a little too close to home. He only wished —

Oh, who was he kidding? It was too late for him to make any kind of wish like the one he wanted to make.

"Brooklyn," he said softly, keeping his tone gentle. "Volunteers at Danny's Haven can't work directly with the troubled teens. Only the counselors can do that, and they have to go through vigorous training and become accredited. It took me —"

"But can't I do something?" she insisted.

He messed up by glancing at her. Her big blue eyes were filled with desperation; he realized he could not tell this girl no. Something about her had his insides stirring with awareness, telling him he should recognize her. Know her. Folding like the proverbial deck of cards, he slumped his shoulders.

"You know what, I'm so backed up on paperwork in my office, it's insane. Maybe if I had an organized assistant helping me file, I could get out into the field more often, and, in return, help more addicts. I know it's not what you had in mind —"

"That's okay," she quickly assured. The smile blooming across her face made his own chest swell with relief. "Anything sounds great."

Ward found himself grinning right back.

19

"Well then . . . great. Here. Let me give you a business card. If you call Danny's Haven and ask to talk to Caren —"

Her brilliant smile faltered. "Why can't I just set it up with you?"

He opened his mouth but no words came. Technically, the state had once listed him as a sexual predator, that's why not. It'd been twelve years since he'd been registered and had completed his treatment program, sure, but if anyone found out about it, he'd still probably worry a couple school administrators for even standing in the middle of a schoolyard alone, talking to a pretty, young woman. And that couldn't possibly be good P.R. for Danny's Haven.

He glanced around uneasily. If Care were still here, nothing about this encounter would be in any way inappropriate. But she was gone, and he would've been right behind her if Brooklyn, who kept looking at him with those begging blue eyes, hadn't waylaid him.

He shifted from one foot to the other and let out an uncomfortable breath.

Care trusted him. She wouldn't mind if he hired on a volunteer — a beautiful, teen girl volunteer — to work directly with him in his office. Would she?

"Umm . . . okay," he said, hesitantly. "I

guess you're hired then. Are you eighteen yet?"

Again, her smile wavered. "I'll be seventeen in three months. Is that a problem?"

Ward shook his head. "No, not at all." The problem would be convincing Care to let him do this in the first place. "We just need permission from a parent and you'll be good to go." I hope.

Brooklyn's grin didn't merely falter this time; it fell flat. "A parent?"

Now he was the one to lift his eyebrows and ask, "Is *that* a problem?"

She bit her lip. Just a little nibble, right at the corner. He'd only seen one other person do that in his lifetime.

"Umm." She cringed. "I don't think my mom would be too . . ."

When her voice trailed off, Ward grinned and finished the sentiment. "Thrilled to let her daughter work at a center where drug addicts hang out? Yeah." He nodded his understanding. "I don't blame her either."

He certainly wouldn't have let his daughter — especially a sweet, too-innocent-looking girl like Brooklyn — anywhere near Danny's Haven. The place might be a refuge for troubled teens but honestly, very few clients who came to their center actually stayed rehabilitated. Some of those flunkies

21

would take one look at Brooklyn and pounce.

"Maybe you could talk to her," she said, her blue eyes alive with her begging plea. "Tell her I won't be near anyone dangerous. You're such a persuasive speaker, I know you could convince her."

He flushed. "Well, thank you, but —"

"I could be safe inside your office the entire time, right?"

"Yeah, sure. But —"

"And someone could walk me to my car when I leave every night."

"Of course. Except —"

"Please, Ward. Please."

I'm already sticking my neck out for you as it is, kid, he wanted to growl. But she kept looking at him with those eyes, and her words continued to echo through his head.

Maybe I wouldn't feel so empty inside where my dad's concerned.

She wanted to do this because of a father she'd never met. He couldn't ignore that. Besides, this wouldn't be the first time he'd made a special case for someone. Probably wouldn't be the last either.

He closed his lashes briefly before giving in. "Okay, fine." He rolled his eyes. "And you say I'm a persuasive speaker." When she grinned triumphantly, he frowned harder. "I'll shoot your mom an email about Danny's Haven, send her a couple of links with information, then explain what I'd like you to do. But if she doesn't agree to it after that, then it's a no-go. All right?"

Nearly vibrating from beaming so brightly, Brooklyn breathed out a rush of oxygen. "All right. Thank you. Thank you so much, Ward. You won't regret it. I promise."

He kind of felt like he already regretted it. But she looked so enthusiastic and happy he let her contagious energy consume him, and he grinned back. "Just, uh, jot down your mom's name and email here." He whipped a pen and piece of scrap paper from his pocket. "And I'll see what I can do."

"Okay." She accepted the sheet and lifted her jean-clad knee to use it as a backstop while she scribbled out his request.

When she handed him her mother's information, he deliberately wrapped his fingers around the note to show her he'd keep it safe. "I'll get in contact with her within the next couple of days."

Brooklyn nodded. "And I'll work on her from my end."

He chuckled. "Sounds good. I hope to see you soon, Brooklyn."

Strangely enough, he meant his words.

The girl exuded an infectious, affectionate attitude. It'd do him good to see her smiling face every few days, keep him optimistic and thinking he could actually save lives.

When she spun away and hurried off, he took a moment to stare after her, feeling achy inside at her departure. There had been something so honest, and pure, and sweet about her. Merely standing in her presence made him feel cleaner. Better. She reminded him of another young female he'd known from a long-ago time.

His smile slipped as nostalgia filled him. Then he shook his head free of bittersweet memories.

Realizing he shouldn't be ogling a teenage girl — he'd probably creep out the teachers and stir up a whole hornets' nest — he cleared his throat and dropped his gaze to the note she'd handed him, his fingers naturally uncurling so he could study the crinkled page.

At first, he barely glanced at the words. His gaze skimmed over what Brooklyn had written until something somewhere in his brain processed her mother's name and gonged with awareness. A split second later, he froze and his attention sharpened.

Ansley Marlow.

His mouth went dry. He hadn't seen that

name in writing for, what — he did a quick calculation in his head — seventeen years, not since the day he'd received the restraining order to stay away from her.

Dear God, had it been that long?

Seeing those letters arranged in that order sent an electric jolt through him. Seventeen years . . .

Wait.

Seventeen years?

Brooklyn's voice echoed through his brain. *I'll be seventeen in three months.*

The air vacated his lungs in a whoosh. He jerked his head up, and his frantic gaze skipped around the courtyard, searching. But the girl, Brooklyn — Ansley Marlow's sixteen-year-old daughter — was gone.

For the second time in the past two minutes, emotion overwhelmed him. He felt like wailing.

"Oh, God," he uttered, beginning to panic. She'd stood right in front of him, smiled at him with Ansley's perfectly formed lips, and he hadn't known who she was.

He couldn't believe it. He'd always thought Ansley's baby would resemble her with her pale hair and stunning brown eyes. But Brooklyn Marlow had his dark locks and his baby blues.

The organ inside his chest expanded,

nearly bursting through his ribcage.

He had a daughter.

CHAPTER TWO

"What I'm trying to say is . . . I want to marry you."

Ansley Marlow squeezed her hands together so hard she cracked a couple knuckles. The man in front of her offered her an uneasy smile as he knelt before her and pulled a black velvet box from his pocket.

Oh, no. He'd even bought her a ring. She wanted to shake her head to deny it but was too frozen to even move her neck. A dreaded chill swept over her, icing her skin.

Lifting the lid of the box to display one of the largest diamonds she'd ever seen, the man in front of her smiled, almost bashfully. "Ansley Ellen Marlow. Would you do me the great honor of becoming my wife?"

She gulped. Poor Preston had been stuttering and fumbling around since he'd shown up at her house five minutes ago. She knew he had something important to say. But she'd kind of been thinking he wanted

27

to end their relationship.

What was worse, she would've preferred it if he'd ended their relationship.

Eyes drawn to the ring he thrust her way, she wilted. The cold sweat coating her turned scorching hot and back to freezing again while she ogled a ring that would no doubt swallow her finger whole. Mercy be. The rock had to span at least three carats large.

"I . . ." Her tongue felt swollen as she tried to speak. No way could she break his heart; it had to be a sin to devastate such a nice man. But no way could she actually marry him.

"I know it's a bit extravagant, which wouldn't be your first preference." He winced as if apologizing for over-spoiling her, which only made her feel worse for being unable to formulate a coherent word. "But as the wife of Dr. Preston B. Jackson, you need the best."

But what if she felt she didn't deserve the best? Of anything.

"Preston, I . . ." She shook her head and drew in a fortifying breath. "You're the dearest man I've ever met. You know that, right? I respect and admire you like no other."

His smiled faltered. "But . . . ?" he said for her.

She sighed. "I love you, Preston. I do. You're my closest friend. But I don't think I'm . . . I'm not *in* love with you."

His face crinkled with confusion before he slowly repeated, "In love?"

She nodded adamantly. "Don't you think, if we were married, there should be feelings? Like, like passion? I mean . . ." She had to blush and glance away before reminding him, "We've never even been intimate."

"I see." He sat back on his haunches, studying her as if he'd just discovered a breakthrough in one of his medical researches. "And you're afraid I wouldn't want to be . . . intimate after we married?"

Actually, she was more afraid he would want that.

Before she could come up with a tactful response, he swept forward, back onto his knees, and grasped her hands in a warm, delicate grip. "Let me guess, you felt like you were in love with Brooklyn's father, am I right?"

Ansley's pity-filled expression fell blank. "I was only fifteen," she rasped, hating the fact she even had to verbalize that. Preston already knew everything she was ever going to tell him about that awful era of her life. But confessing a teenage pregnancy always made her ashamed and defiant in equal parts.

She hated the social stigma placed on her as if she'd been some wild, party-animal floozie just as much as she hated feeling as if she should be embarrassed about having the most amazing daughter ever.

"Ah." Preston murmured. He patted her hand with sympathy. "So you think since it happened when you were so young, it can't be trusted?"

She wasn't sure of that answer, so she remained mute.

His fingers squeezed affectionately around hers. "Well, I agree."

With a frown, she blurted, "You do?"

Preston nodded. "Of course. I thought I was in love with my first wife. But Rachel left me for another man fifteen years into our marriage. You thought you were in love with Brooklyn's father, yet he left as soon as you told him you were pregnant."

She opened her mouth to defend a man she hadn't seen in seventeen years. But she had no idea how to defend such a brutal fact, so she pressed her lips together and remained silent . . . again.

"It's a fleeting sensation, this in love

you're talking about. It can't be trusted, and shouldn't be trusted. What we have is real. It's true companionship. And it's dependable and honest. I think you and I — and Brooklyn — could make a peaceful, happy life together. Just the three of us. We could be content. A family."

Family.

The delicious word lured her like nothing else.

A full, complete family was all she'd ever wanted.

When she made to speak, though, he interrupted her again, even set his fingers over her lips to hush her. "I'll be honest with you, Ansley. I'm not looking for a love match this time around. I want a partner at my side to share my life with. That's all. I'm lonely, and we get on well together. We could succeed where so many others who think they're passionately in love have failed, where we've both already failed with other people."

Ansley blew out a breath, wanting to scowl because he made such a talented, persuasive argument. His deal actually sounded appealing — tempting — when marrying him was the last thing she wanted. She didn't fit into his world. A single mother struggling to pay her bills every month knew nothing about becoming the wife of an affluent surgeon.

But a family.

Oh, a family with a mother-father unit and the perfect daughter would be so nice. It'd be the American dream come true. Her dream come true.

Besides, Brooklyn really seemed to like Preston. Maybe for her child, she could consider his proposition. And even after Brooklyn left in a few years for college, companionship in a content, secure, peaceful relationship sounded a heck of a lot better than lonely nights watching TV by herself.

"I need to think about this," she fumbled out her answer. "I need to talk to Brooklyn. I need . . . a little time." She felt lame repeating her sentiment three different ways but she couldn't help it. This was a significant, life-altering choice he'd just asked her to make.

Preston nodded and leaned forward to give her a chaste kiss on the cheek. "I think that's wise. No important decision should be made on the spur of the moment. So . . . mull it over, weigh your options and decide what's best for you and Brooklyn. I'm sure you'll make the right choice."

She smiled, actually reassured by his ready

acceptance of her hesitance. It reminded her of all the reasons she liked him in the first place. He really was a dear man. He didn't even seem upset when she nearly came right out and told him she didn't feel a spark of chemistry toward him, which made her blush like a nincompoop for even thinking that's what two people had to have in order to get married. There was more — much more — to a relationship than silly sparks.

Sparks were pretty much the only thing she'd had with . . . with Brooklyn's father, and just look how awful that had turned out. She hadn't seen him for almost two decades.

Preston was right. Sparks definitely couldn't be trusted.

Companionship was what mattered. Family. Peace. She didn't want to grow old alone and die by herself. Maybe she could give marriage a try. And since Preston was the only candidate she would even consider for the position of husband . . .

"Oh, before I forget," Preston broke into her thoughts. Closing the ring box with a negligent snap, he pocketed it and drew out a handful of pamphlets. "A Harvard-graduate rep was in the office today, and he had some reading material on their medical program. I thought Brooklyn would be interested in glancing through these since she expressed an interest in becoming a pediatrician someday."

A thin laugh escaped Ansley as she took the pamphlets. "Thanks, but . . . there's no way I could get Brooklyn through Harvard. Even after all the scholarships she'll no doubt receive, it would be nearly impossible to afford such a pricey —"

"It'd be possible if I was around," Preston said quietly.

Swallowing, Ansley glanced up as her face drained of warmth.

What was he saying? Was he telling her he'd pay Brooklyn's way through Harvard if she married him? Unease swamped her. Were these pamphlets plan B in case she turned her nose up at his ring? She didn't want to be paid off, especially when he used her daughter as leverage. She didn't want —

His good-natured laugh made her blink. "But what am I saying? There's still a couple of years for her to make up her mind of where she wants to go. Since the rep just thrust these at me, it got me thinking about her future, that's all. Sorry, sweetheart. Didn't mean to work ahead of myself there."

Ansley studied him a moment longer. He didn't appear to have an ulterior motive behind his words. His eyes held no hidden agenda. Maybe he really had given the pamphlets to her in innocent excitement, not even thinking how she could construe his meaning.

He grinned innocuously. "She might have fun looking through them though."

Ansley nodded, her smile trembling with effort as she slipped the brochures from his hand. "I'm sure she will. She loves planning ahead."

Preston nodded as well. "That's what I figured." Still kneeling somewhat awkwardly before her, he pushed to his feet, levering his hands onto his knees and straightening. His joints popped as he rose, reminding her he was thirteen years her senior, which brought up another reason she'd been hesitant about dating him in the first place. People would think she was a gold digger and he was her sugar daddy.

She was so tired of being just another disappointing stigma in strangers' judgmental eyes. For once, it'd be nice to do something people actually approved of. That her parents approved of.

"Well," Preston said, and then paused as if at a loss for words.

The front door flew open, saving them both from coming up with awkward after-proposal conversation. Ansley lurched up from the couch where she'd been sitting and stopped next to Preston.

Brooklyn rushed inside, a flurry of movement and color. "Mom, you will not believe what happened today." She carelessly flung her book bag into an armchair and unwrapped her scarf as she hurried forward. The front door fell shut behind her, nestling the three of them inside together.

Like a family.

"Brooklyn," Ansley wheezed, setting her hand over her thudding heart. "Thank goodness you're home. I needed to talk to you."

She darted a quick glance at Preston. He smiled rather smugly before clearing his throat and stepping back. "Well," he said. "I guess I'll leave you two ladies to your discussions. Brooklyn." He nodded formally at the teen.

"Hey, Dr. Jackson," she greeted with an affectionate grin but immediately turned back to Ansley, grasping both her hands. "Mom, seriously. I'm so stoked. This group called Danny's Haven visited our school today and gave this really cool presentation about . . ."

As she rattled on, Ansley couldn't take her eyes off Preston while he quietly made his way to the door. He opened it and paused, glancing at her one last time before he nodded a farewell and slipped into the darkening evening. The latch had barely clicked when Brooklyn's excited chatter made her frown and focus on her child.

"Why are you coming in so late?" she interrupted to ask. She usually got off work well after the time her daughter got home. It was rare when she beat Brooklyn through the door.

Brooklyn waved an unconcerned hand. "Oh, Kelsey's boyfriend dumped her today during fourth hour. Totally out of the blue. She's majorly bummed, so I spent some time with her, telling her how much better off she'll be without him."

Ansley smiled, proud of her daughter. "That was really nice of you, honey. I'm glad you support your friends so well."

"Yeah, whatever. Back to what I was saying. This guy's name is Ward Gemmell, and he's really cool. He said —"

"What!" The word strangled in Ansley's throat as that name echoed through her head. "Wait, wait, wait. Back up and restart from the beginning. What in God's name are you talking about?" There was no way she'd heard that right, no way Brooklyn had actually said the name Ansley swore she'd just said.

Brooklyn sighed. "Mom, concentrate. This is really important to me."

Ansley licked her suddenly dry lips and nodded. She wasn't about to miss a word her daughter said this time around . . . because it was really important to her too.

"I'm listening."

"This group called Danny's Haven came to the school today to talk about drug abuse. They gave this amazing presentation about how they help people clean up their lives. It was so inspiring, Mom, you should've been there and heard the things they do."

Ansley nodded vaguely, her skin buzzing with anxious awareness as she waited for that name to pop from her daughter's mouth again. And since drugs had been mentioned, she had a sinking suspicion it would be coming soon.

"So I talked with one of the counselors afterward, and he said I could volunteer at Danny's Haven, like help him with some paperwork in his office and stuff. But I need your permission first."

A nervous laugh trilled from Ansley's throat. "I . . . I . . ." She shook her head, unable to concentrate. What had her daughter just asked her? "What . . ." After licking her dry lips again, she took a deep breath.

Focus, Ansley. Listen.

"What did you say this counselor's name was?" She hedged the question slowly, cautiously, her nerves finally steady enough she could breathe normally again.

That was until Brooklyn went and answered, "Ward. Ward Gemmell. But he prefers to go by Ward." She grinned goofily. "He says being called mister makes him feel like he's wearing a tie."

Nodding dumbly, Ansley tried to keep her face expressionless and void of all the emotions and thoughts afflicting her. Questions sprang to her lips but she couldn't settle her rattled unease enough to ask a single one. She could only stand there and listen to her daughter gush about her own father.

"He gave the best speech ever. I guess he actually did drugs when he was younger, and it was super hard for him to quit. He talked about some of the wrong choices he made when he was young and how long it took him to get clean. It was so inspiring. For realz. It made me want to do what he does, and help people. So I talked to him afterward and —"

"You talked to him?" Ansley choked out, her eyes nearly bursting from their sockets. A second later, she slammed her hand over her chest, stole another moment to regain her composure and dropped her fingers, clearing her throat. "He's truly clean now?"

Brooklyn nodded ardently. "Yes, you don't have to worry about that at all. He had to go through vigorous training and get accredited to become a counselor. There's no way he could keep his job if he wasn't clean. Plus, he said I wouldn't be allowed to work directly with any of the addicts, so you don't have to worry about that, either. I'd just be in an office, assisting with paperwork, probably filing and organizing the whole time. It'd be completely safe."

Under any other circumstances, Brooklyn's safety would be Ansley's first concern. But her thoughts were so scattered and unorganized, rank of importance grew sadly under par.

Right now, what mattered most was, "Does he know who . . . who you are?"

Brooklyn blinked and sent her a baffled look. "Uh . . . yeah, I told him my dad had done drugs if that's what you mean."

Ansley's shoulders eased fractionally. From listening to Brooklyn, she had to assume her daughter remained clueless about who he was to her personally. She wasn't sure if that knowledge relieved her or only made her more restless.

". . . So I gave him your name and email address to contact you about —"

Gagging on oxygen, Ansley pressed a hand back to her tight chest, hoping she wasn't having a heart attack. Thirty-two was too young to die.

"You ga— you gave him my name?"

"And email address," Brooklyn added, bobbing her head. "He said he needs your permission to let me volunteer since I'm not eighteen."

A loud, abrupt rush of buzzing air screamed through her ears.

So he had to know who Brooklyn was then. She wondered what his reaction had been. Or maybe he'd already known about his daughter, surreptitiously keeping track of her through the years, biding his time to approach her until the right moment.

But why would he sneak around before contacting Brooklyn?

She felt so confused.

When Brooklyn looked at her with her father's blue eyes and pleaded, "So, please, please, please can I volunteer at Danny's Haven?" Ansley had no idea how to answer.

"I . . ." She shook her head, trying to clear it. Concentrate, focus. Answer the question. "I don't know, honey. I'll have to think about this." Right after she remembered how to think again.

"Okay. That's fine." Instead of pushing, Brooklyn merely nodded, though her eyes remained bright with hope. She took a deep breath, her face glowing with pleasure as if she felt she'd already gotten her way. "So . . . what did you want to talk to me about?"

Again, Ansley shook her head. "What?"

Brooklyn rolled her eyes and laughed. "When I came in, you said you needed to talk to me about something."

"Oh." Frowning, trying to concentrate, and failing, Ansley sank her fingers through her hair and rubbed at her aching scalp. "I can't remember anymore."

CHAPTER THREE

"Care, I need to talk to you. Now."

Ward blew into his supervisor's office, forgetting to knock as he immediately began to pace the floor in front of her desk, barely noticing she was busy on the phone.

"I . . . I'm sorry, George," she sputtered into the receiver she held to her ear as she pushed from her chair, jerking to her feet. "Can I call you back? I think I have an emergency here." She gaped at Ward as she hung up. "Oh my God. Have you been crying?"

"I don't know. Maybe." Too distracted to answer properly, Ward ripped his hand through his hair.

"Well, what happened?"

"I . . ." He glanced at her, and the words froze in his throat.

Sucking in a deep breath, he closed the door to her office when he noticed it standing wide open. Care might know every deep, dark secret from his past, but she was the only one, and he preferred to keep it that way.

Once he closeted them alone, he turned to face her fully, and then he rushed out the words before he lost his nerve. "I just met my daughter."

Care straightened and set her hands flat against the top of her desk. "Say what?"

He nodded. "An . . . Ansley had the baby, I guess. It was a girl. Her name's Brooklyn. And she attends J. Edgar Hoover High School." He cradled his pounding head in his palms as his own words echoed back to his ears and resounded through his brain. "Oh my God."

Questions that had plagued him for years had been answered today, so quickly, so unexpectedly. It left him reeling. Queasy.

"Oh my God," he wheezed again. "I can't breathe."

Care darted around her desk. "Well, sit down before you have a panic attack and pass out." She pointed to a chair even as she hurried to him.

He slumped down. "Too late." Panic clouded his vision until he could see only grey, breathe in only murky, thick drudges of grey. Bowing his head and clenching his eyes closed, he let out a moan of distress.

Care set a warm hand on the back of his neck and began to knead the tense muscles. "Just breathe," she instructed in her calm, maternal voice.

He focused on the rhythm of her fingers working his neck muscles and the tone of her soothing instructions. As he sucked in oxygen and relaxed, he realized just how much he loved this woman and wished she could've been his mother. His life might've turned out so differently if he'd known her when he was younger.

Actually, there was no might've to it. It would have been different. If he'd had a mother to love him —

Thinking of parents and their lacking duties, though, made tears flood his eyelashes.

"I stood there and stared her straight in the eye. We spoke for almost five minutes. And I didn't even know who she was." When his voice broke, he gave up on talking and buried his face between his knees.

He was a parent and he hadn't recognized his own child. Even his awful mother had been better than that. The agony of it crippled him. Ashamed and humiliated, he wanted to wilt into nothing and disappear from the world, from himself. But with each anguished breath that hurled its way through his body, he wilted nowhere and remained exactly who he was, alive and as corporeal as he'd been the moment before he'd learned of Brooklyn Marlow's existence.

No matter how much he wished to undo what had been done and escape it all, this was now his life. And he'd have to find a way to deal with it.

Care didn't say anything, bless her, she merely let him lean against her leg and sob on her slacks while she stroked his head.

"What do I do?" he asked when he'd drained himself of enough self-pity to talk again. Straightening, he shifted away from Care and wiped at his damp face before glancing up to seek all the answers from his beloved mentor.

Instead of telling him what to do however, Care arched a pensive eyebrow. "What do you want to do?"

He snorted out a bitter laugh. "Go back to being eighteen and do it right the first time."

She smiled sadly and shrugged. "Well, that's not an option, now is it?"

With a frown, he muttered, "You're not helping."

"Ward, honestly." Irritation laced her voice. "Just think it through. What do you tell one of your teens when they hit a fork in the road and need to make the right decision?"

After thinking about it from that perspective, Ward let out a breath. "I tell them to come up with all the responsible paths there are to take, weigh the pros and cons of each, and then decide which one is best for everyone involved."

Care lifted her hands. "Then, there you have it."

Ward scowled. Really, her evasive answers sometimes exasperated him to no end. But in all honesty, it was one of the features he liked best about her. She never pampered or coddled, never went the easy way and simply told him what he wanted to hear. She made him work for his answers and come to his own conclusion. That tough-edged quality about her always induced him to strive harder and find a way to impress her.

Nodding, he blew out another breath and pushed to his feet. "I guess I've got some serious thinking to do then."

She smiled, approval crinkling into the wrinkles lining her aging eyes. "That you do. And don't forget it's your night to supervise the supper crowd."

"But —" For the first time in the seven years since he'd started at Danny's Haven,

47

Ward opened his mouth to protest.

The center stayed open twenty-four hours a day to house any teenager needing a safe place to temporarily find refuge. The counselors worked regular nine-to-five hours but they all took a turn staying late to stick around in case someone needed immediate assistance, because let's face it, troubling issues didn't always wait around until regular working hours to arise.

Ward had worked more than his fair share of overtime, staying late. He probably worked more overtime than he did regular time. He felt he deserved one night of relief.

He'd actually expected his oh-so-beloved mentor to suggest he take the evening off to deal with his personal crisis.

But when Caren arched a brow, silently daring him to argue, he snapped his mouth shut and silently nodded. "I'll be here."

Physically at least. His head was miles away, however. He was so lost in his thoughts he plowed into a sixteen-year-old girl as he left Care's office.

"Sorry." Snaking out a hand, he caught her arm so he couldn't knock her down. "Didn't see you there." His fingers barely wrapped around her thin limb, though, before he realized who he was handling.

Tara had appeared on the front steps of

Danny's Haven about six months ago with two bruised eyes and a broken wrist. After hearing her story in group therapy, Ward had learned she'd been molested by more than one male family member since she was thirteen. She'd turned to drugs as a way to cope.

These days, she was a regular at the center, sometimes camping out for nights at a time. She'd come a long way since the first moment he'd seen her. She used to be so jumpy she'd yelp aloud whenever he looked like he might touch her.

Keeping that in mind, Ward released her as soon as she was steady, jerking his hands back respectfully. "You okay?"

Seemingly unbothered by the contact, Tara nodded and smiled up at him. "I'm fine."

Proud to see health and lucidity and even a measure of contentment in her brown eyes, he grinned back and stepped aside to let her pass. Yet watching her reminded him of his own daughter. His chest tightened with achy pressure.

Brooklyn had seemed healthy, drug-free, and very content herself. That pleased him. A lot. Made him wonder if she would still be that well-adjusted if he'd been around her all these years and had played a part in her upbringing. Brows crinkling with his troubled thoughts, he turned in the direction of his office.

"Hey, Ward," a group of boys called when he reached the main commons area. "Want to watch a movie with us? We got a Marvel marathon going on."

He barely glanced over as he shook his head. "Not tonight. I've got . . . paperwork. I'll be in my office if anyone needs me."

He escaped inside before anyone could answer or argue. Shutting the door, he pressed his back against it and ran his hands over his face. If someone had reached into his head, squeezed a fistful of his brain and bounced it against the inside of his skull a few times, he didn't think he could feel any more scrambled than he did now.

"Come up with all the responsible paths to take," he said aloud, reminding himself of his priorities.

The two main paths were obvious: either ignore today and pretend it had never happened, or react to it.

Ignoring it wasn't even a possibility. Brooklyn hadn't seemed like the type to sit on her hands and wait for him to contact her. She'd been too energized not to want a follow-up. She would contact him if he didn't do something. And honestly, he didn't want to ignore this. He wanted to know his daughter. He wanted to do the right thing. He wanted to see how Ansley was faring these days.

A shudder of yearning worked through him. He beat it back down and concentrated on the girl. His daughter. He couldn't think about Ansley right now. But the slip of paper in his pocket with her name on it burned against his hip.

Obtaining her email address was the closest he'd been to her in seventeen years. Heart thumping hard, he pulled the note out and let his thumb sweep wistfully over her name.

Since he decided ignoring wasn't an option, the next logical path would be to get hold of his daughter's mother. He refused to go behind Ansley's back, which narrowed his options to this one email address.

He'd already memorized her user name yet he eyed it again, unable to stop studying Brooklyn's penmanship. As the only way to reach Ansley, an email seemed the best path to take. Maybe it was the cowardly path, but that suited him. He felt pretty weak in the knees as it was. But honestly, he had no idea how she would receive his reappearance in her life. He didn't want to crowd her, upset her, or scare her, and an email would be the least invasive way to contact her.

She'd probably reject him. He'd deserve it, but he had to find out. Seventeen years of wondering was too long.

He couldn't get the image of Brooklyn's longing expression out of his head when she'd looked him in the eye and begged him to make her a volunteer so she could feel closer to her father. She ached to know him. And he ached to know her.

To give his daughter what she craved, he had to find a tactful way to make that possible, even if it upset Ansley, which is what he'd spent the last seventeen years trying not to do.

So an email it would be.

He moved toward his desk and set the paper with her information gently beside his keyboard and atop a mammoth pile of unfiled folders. After logging into his account, he began typing the most important letter of his life.

An hour later, he wiped his tired, strained eyes and sat back in his chair to re-read what he'd composed.

Dear Ansley,
I met Brooklyn today. I'm sorry I didn't realize who she was until after we had

talked and she was already gone. I work at a drug-counseling clinic to help conflicted teens, and my organization came to her high school to give a preventive presentation. She approached me afterward, wanting to volunteer at Danny's Haven where I work.

She gave me your email address to contact you and tell you a little about our program, hoping that would help coax you into agreeing to let her volunteer. I didn't look at the information she gave me until after she'd left. To say the least, it was a shock to read your name.

I know nothing I type in this letter will ever aptly describe the experience of meeting her, but I think you've done an amazing job raising a bright, caring, beautiful young lady. Since I have straightened up my life, I would be honored to acknowledge her as my daughter if that was agreeable with you.

But I understand completely if you're not comfortable with that arrangement, and I will respect whatever decision you make. If you wish to respond to me, I'm leaving all my contact information below.

I hope you are well.

Best regards, Ward.

He wasn't sure how many times he'd back-spaced and reworded but his stiff, aching fingers told him it had been plenty. Drumming the overused digits against his chin, he studied the note and wondered if he should've typed the words "my daughter." They sounded so . . . permanent. There was no taking them back.

But daughters were fairly permanent things. He kept it as-is and read it again, wincing as he came to the valediction.

"Best regards? I hope you are well? Seriously, this has to be the most formal piece of garbage I've ever written."

It sounded like he was addressing a complete stranger. But how familiar should he get? Though seriously, why he was even stressing over the note was a mystery. Ansley was probably going to press delete as soon as she saw the sender's name. No way would she accept a letter from him.

He rubbed his face, giving up for the evening, and decided to sleep on it. One of Care's most-used catch phrases echoed through his head about how no important decision should be made on the spur of the moment. And this definitely fell under the heading of important.

In the morning, he'd read the letter again. After a good night's sleep — or most likely very little sleep, if he wanted to be honest with himself — his head would be clearer and he could edit and revise to perfection.

Sliding his mouse up, he clicked on save, only to realize the save button sat next to the link he actually pressed. Zipping his gaze to the button under his cursor, praying he hadn't deleted the whole thing, Ward gasped. Color drained from his face when he realized he'd chosen the send command.

"Oh no."

This couldn't be good. He hadn't even told her how long he'd been clean or how she shouldn't be worried about him ever resorting to drugs again. He hadn't mentioned how he had thought about her every day for the past seventeen years and how he would never be able to apologize enough for ruining her life. He hadn't promised he'd die before he ever hurt her again.

His stomach roiled with unease.

He wasn't ready for this, wasn't ready for whatever response she gave. She'd been the forgiving type back when he'd first known her. But he wasn't sure if he could handle hearing any degree of forgiveness from her either. He deserved to be damned for all eternity.

Then again, how could he live with himself knowing how much she hated him if she didn't forgive him?

No matter how she reacted, he told himself he would survive. He had lived through rough times before; he could do it again. He just hoped he'd be able to bear his suffering with some degree of dignity.

CHAPTER FOUR

Ansley knew her daughter too well. Whenever Brooklyn wanted something desperately, she planned a detailed strategy of attack. She didn't come out full force and beg non-stop, because in return, she knew her mother too well. Ansley had never fallen for annoying, repetitive begging on principle alone.

So Brooklyn waited patiently. She slipped in sly references to her desires, slowly and steadily working on Ansley from all angles and picking her way in toward the heart of her wishes until she had her mother surrounded with well thought-out reasons for giving in.

But this evening, every mention Brooklyn made about volunteering at that rehabilitation center grated on Ansley's already raw nerves.

For instance, when Brooklyn said as she helped set the table for supper, "You know,

I think I'm old enough to start doing something constructive with my life," Ansley clenched her teeth and burned her finger from a splash of the spaghetti sauce she'd been stirring too vigorously.

"Curse it!" She stuck her stinging pinkie into her mouth, the flavor of oregano and tomato sauce washing across her tongue.

"You okay?" Brooklyn paused with a plate in her hand as she glanced over.

Ansley wasn't sure if she'd ever be okay again. But she nodded and yanked her finger free. "I'm fine."

Brooklyn nodded and continued. "I mean, don't you think it'd be good for my developing personality to volunteer some of my time to a worthy cause?"

Glad her back faced her daughter so Brooklyn couldn't see her expression, Ansley rolled her eyes. The kid's personality seemed developed to the max already, if anyone wanted her opinion.

"I think I'd feel better about myself if —"

"Can we please not talk about this right now," Ansley snapped.

Brooklyn fell silent, making Ansley wince. She swallowed back her apology, her spine aching with the tight rigid way she held it. Closing her eyes as she stirred in a steady, monotonous manner, she took a deep breath, calming herself.

"Mom?"

Her baby sounded so concerned, Ansley opened her eyes and glanced over her shoulder. "Yes?"

Forehead crinkling as she studied her, Brooklyn asked, "Are you okay?"

Ansley swallowed, unable to answer. Should she tell Brooklyn everything right now? Or should she wait a few days, get some advice from friends first? Maybe she should never tell Brooklyn at all. Ward obviously hadn't told her; maybe he didn't want her to know for some life-threatening reason, meaning Ansley shouldn't tell her either.

Holding her tongue, she finally bobbed her head with a jerky nod. "Yes, I . . ." She forced a reassuring smile. "I'm fine. Sorry. I just . . ." Rubbing at her temple, she told the God's honest truth. "I have a small headache."

Who wouldn't at a time like this?

Brooklyn's brows lowered in a suspicious manner. "So, you didn't have a fight with Dr. Jackson or anything?"

For a split-second, Ansley had to stop and think who Dr. Jackson was. Then her eyes flared. Preston! His proposal. She'd yet to divulge how he wanted to marry her. She watched Brooklyn arrange the silverware beside each plate before she swung her head back and forth.

"No. No. I . . . we didn't have a fight at all. In fact . . ."

No words came. She wasn't sure why, but she couldn't say it. Here was the perfect opening to announce his proposal and see what Brooklyn thought of the idea, but her tongue stalled out. Instead of revealing anything, she frowned. "You still call him Dr. Jackson."

Brooklyn shrugged. "Yeah. So?"

"So, don't you feel comfortable enough around him to call him Preston yet?"

Another shrug ensued. "I don't know. I guess I could. But he's never told me to use his first name."

"Hmm." Ansley frowned thoughtfully. Odd that. Why hadn't she ever noticed the formality between the two before? Maybe the three of them wouldn't make as perfect a family as Preston had insinuated.

The phone ringing made her jump and drop her stirring spoon into the sauce. As it disappeared into the red juice, Brooklyn leapt toward the wall-mount receiver.

"I'll get it."

Ansley whirled around and opened her mouth to screech, "No!" but stopped herself at the last moment. It could be Ward. Or Preston. Or no one of consequence.

Heart thumping in her throat, she watched, holding her breath, as Brooklyn picked up. "Hello?" A second later, sympathy ruled her expression. "Hey, Kelsey. We're just getting ready to eat. How're you doing?"

Shoulders slumping with relief, Ansley turned back to the sauce and fished the spoon out as her daughter chatted with her best friend. They talked most of the way through supper. From listening to Brooklyn's end of the conversation, sixteen-year-old Kelsey wasn't dealing with her breakup very well at all.

Usually, Ansley discouraged it when Brooklyn talked on the phone while they ate. But tonight, Ansley welcomed the interruption. Plus, Kelsey seemed to need her.

Ansley liked knowing her daughter was such a good, supportive friend and could be counted on as a shoulder to cry against. Before this was over, Ansley feared she may need a good shoulder for that very thing. She had no idea what to do about either development that had sprung into her life less than an hour ago.

Stuffing noodles down her throat and tasting nothing, she finished her meal, feeling disconnected from reality. On autopilot, she cleared the table and washed the dishes. Brooklyn finally disconnected from her call just as Ansley set the last dried glass in the cupboard.

"Hey, I got out of kitchen duty," Brooklyn noticed with an approving beam. "Good timing, huh?"

Ansley grinned even as she rubbed a circle on her forehead.

"So, I don't have any homework tonight. Do you want to watch some TV together? I think there's a new episode of —"

"Oh, not tonight, honey," Ansley interrupted on a mumble. She waved her hand vaguely, trying to think up a good excuse.

Brooklyn's face wrinkled with concern. "Is the headache another bad one?"

Ansley nodded mutely, clasping onto the lie as if it were a life jacket. Her head did ache but the pain hadn't quite reached migraine status. Still, she massaged the side of one temple. "I think I'll just lie down for a while." When her daughter nodded with an understanding look of pity, Ansley turned away, feeling guilty for not being honest and up front.

As she escaped to her room, Brooklyn called after her. "Take one of your pills this time."

"Yes, mother," Ansley called back with a teasing grin.

Since she'd moved out of her parents' house eleven years ago when Brooklyn was five, she and Brooklyn had become closer than normal mother and daughter. A team, they were two against the world and often protected each other. Ansley adored that aspect of their relationship as much as she regretted it. Brooklyn probably wouldn't have needed to grow so responsible so early in life if she'd had more than one parent in it.

She wanted to hate Ward Gemmell for that.

But she couldn't.

As soon as she shut the door to her room, she dashed straight to her laptop she'd left on her nightstand and crawled onto her bed, pulling it onto her knees with trembling hands.

After booting up, she clicked into the internet and racked her brain.

What had Brooklyn called the center where he worked? Denny's House? Donny's? Danny's? Danny's! That was it.

She typed in Danny's House and immediately found the picture of a castle in England, a music band's website, and a steak restaurant.

No rehabilitation center.

Hmm.

It had been Danny's House, hadn't it? No, now that she thought about it, that didn't sound quite right, but she couldn't ask Brooklyn for the correct name. That would produce a bunch of questions she didn't want to answer, and she certainly didn't want to give her daughter false hope about volunteering at a drug clinic.

Wait. Being a drug clinic, its name had something with refuge or shelter. Retreat? Sanctuary? Haven . . . Haven!

Danny's Haven.

She typed Danny's Haven into her search program and the first hit came up with a rehabilitation center located on the other side of the city.

Her fingers shook as she clicked on the link.

Immediately, she saw him.

The breath rushed from her lungs.

He didn't look at all like the eighteen-year-old boy she used to know, yet the jolt of awareness ricocheting through her system told her without a doubt she was staring at an image of Ward Gemmell. Her skin burned with vitality as if awakening abruptly from a deep sleep.

He took up about twenty percent of the

photo placed just under the main banner and navigation bar. In an action shot, he wore a T-shirt and baggy, knee-length shorts as he jumped up, one hand held high to block a ball the teenage boy in front of him was shooting at the basket behind him. A gleam of sweat coated his brow, and his dark hair clumped together, showing how wet it must be.

The caption under the picture didn't label him by name; it merely said, "At Danny's Haven, we offer one-on-one personalized contact with the teens who come to us."

She smiled slightly at the basketball pun even as her gaze strayed back to Ward.

Eager to enlarge the photograph and see him a little more clearly, she snuck a glance toward the door, hoping Brooklyn didn't barge in, and then ran her cursor over his face, which had aged quite handsomely. She clicked on him, but the picture link led her to a different page, where no photograph of him adorned the new screen.

Disappointment tasted like acid in her mouth. She swallowed it down and browsed a while longer, searching for any reference of his name she could find. In the contact page, she found him again among a handful of in-house counselors. Unable to help herself, she entered his page. Not much information had been attributed him, nothing personal, just his accreditations — which made her lungs feel tight with a strange pride to read all he'd accomplished. An email address and his office number were listed under that, and a YouTube video had been embedded to the right. She clicked on it, wishing maybe —

There he was.

This time, the breath caught in her throat, making her chest burn. He'd become a grown man, yet the rigid set of his body as he sat in a chair on a stage not far from the podium in what looked like a high school auditorium where an older woman greeted the students before them made her remember him as the teen she used to know. His shoulders curled in as if he felt he was about to be reprimanded and was braced for the punishment. He had sat exactly the same way through every Bible study meeting he'd ever attended.

She found herself skipping ahead, fast forwarding until the woman talking sat down and Ward pushed to his feet. Ansley punched play.

Leaning forward slightly, he spoke into the microphone and greeted everyone with a voice she didn't remember. It had grown deeper, clearer, which told her she was staring at a stranger. But she couldn't look away, couldn't stop remembering.

"I started doing drugs when I was thirteen." He started his presentation with an abashed shrug before flashing a grin which made her stomach flip. He still had the same breathtaking grin of the boy she once knew. "Wasn't very good at it though. The first time I inhaled marijuana — and oh yeah, I inhaled — I was sick to my stomach. Puked up everything inside me. My friends never let me live that one down."

Brooklyn's laugh came from the living room, rattling through the closed door of Ansley's bedroom. She jumped with a guilty start and lowered the volume on her laptop so her daughter couldn't hear. Straining closer to the speaker on the side, she listened intently.

"I was what you'd call a punk. Thought I needed to try everything at least once. But I wasn't very good at that either." The students listening to Ward chuckled at his humor. Ansley smiled longingly, her ribcage heaving when she gulped in oxygen. "My crew named me Slammer because I was the one that always got caught."

His admission earned another laugh from the crowd.

On the screen, Ward frowned. "Oh, you

don't believe me, huh? Here, let me give you an example. We found these rotten old vegetables in a dumpster behind this restaurant one time and thought it'd be fun to throw them at passing cars on the street. The three guys before me took a turn and smacked their cars straight at the driver's side window. So I clutched my smelly head of slimy lettuce, darted out of the alley and hammered the next vehicle to pass, bulls eye . . . only to realize it was a cop car."

His audience tittered yet again. Even Ansley found herself covering her mouth to hide a smile. She could actually picture him doing that. It filled her with painful nostalgia, and her grin died the same moment his did.

"We won't go into any of the other illegal things I was caught doing. To say the least, I was quite the hoodlum."

He drifted silently for a moment, as if replaying old times through his head. She wondered if he was remembering her at all when he leaned forward and said, "I fell in love during the heaviest time of my addiction."

Her breath caught in her throat as the video zoomed in on his face to show the silly, love-struck smile brightening his features. She told herself he couldn't be talking about her, he wouldn't —

"Sweetest girl you could ever meet," he murmured. "Pretty face, beautiful soul. She was it. I'm telling you, fellas. If you ever meet a girl like this, you'll know what I'm talking about. She ruins you for any other female out there. She's just . . . perfect."

He sighed, looking lost in sweet memories. "I'll never forget the first day I met her. My buddies and I were bored and broke. Nothing to smoke. As we were strolling down the sidewalk looking for some way to get into trouble and not get caught, we passed this church. Two of my friends began to banter back and forth, daring the other to go up and knock on the door, then ask if God was home whenever someone answered. Well, I got tired of listening to them chicken out, so I announced I'd do it."

Ansley's stomach dropped into her knees. He was talking about her. She couldn't believe it, couldn't believe he was telling their story. Having never heard it from his point of view, she turned up the volume as much as she dared.

"So I strolled up to the front door and balled my hand to knock. But . . . I don't know, for some reason, I paused. Instead of knocking, I reached out and tried the handle. When I found it unlocked, I pulled it open and glanced over my shoulder at my friends, silently asking if anyone dared me to go inside."

He paused dramatically, and Ansley found herself sitting forward, watching his face.

"They all waved me on, so I stepped inside a church for the first time in my life." He took another deep breath. "I thought lightning was going to strike me dead. I kid you not. I just stood there, frozen, right inside the doorway, waiting to die. But nothing happened; lightning never struck and no one came to shoo me out. It was just me standing like a moron inside the front lobby of a church. It had been a warm day, the middle of summer, so I soaked in the nice air conditioning and glanced around to see exactly what a church looked like on the inside.

"There were so many little trinkets and small tables, pictures on the wall, just sitting around for anyone to take. I began to think I needed to steal something, to show my friends I could, you know. Build me up some decent street cred. That's when I spotted a plastic jar full of money with a little sign taped around it asking for donations to help save some girl with cancer."

Ward's shoulders slumped as he glanced toward each far corner of the auditorium.

"Yeah," he said, his voice a regretful confession. "I was going to take that. You know you've hit rock bottom when you plan to steal from dying children. But salvation came in the form of a pretty little blonde. While I was trying to creep stealthily toward that jar, someone exited a hall from my right and spoke behind me, asking if I was there to join the bible study group."

He chuckled slightly. Watching him, Ansley drifted into the past, remembering when she had asked him that very question. He'd jumped and swung around so quickly, he looked guiltier than she'd ever seen anyone look. And now she knew why.

"I swear, I almost had a heart attack. I whirled around to run but . . . then I saw her." Nodding, he glanced at his audience. "Most beautiful girl ever. Instead of running, I just stood there . . . like a moron — again — unable to stop staring. At first, I thought she was an angel. I wondered if maybe lightning had struck me, and I'd died and gone to heaven. Then she smiled, and I suddenly didn't care if I was dead or alive. As long as she didn't disappear, life was good."

"You're just in time," Ansley remembered telling him. And still, he'd stood there and stared at her. It had made her warm in the belly. Flushing, she hooked her thumb over her shoulder and pointed. "We're all back here, ready to start." She'd turned away to lead him to the meeting, hoping he would follow, because honestly, he'd been the cutest boy to ever attend one of the bible study sessions.

"When she walked off, I don't know why, I just followed her. I would've followed her anywhere. I pulled to a stop when we reached the room she'd led me to, though, startled to find half a dozen other teens seated around a folding table and a man with a white collar. Again, I almost turned tail and ran, but the girl looked at me. She pulled out a chair for me to sit beside her. So . . . I sat.

"I went back the next week, and the next week, just so I could see her. I know it was crazy. I sat through an hour-long bible study class every week that summer . . . for a girl. But oh, was she worth it. She'd share her bible with me, and we'd have to scoot closer together to read from it. Sometimes our knees would brush and my heart would hammer so hard through my chest I was sure everyone in the room could hear it." He shook his head. "Being around her was better — more powerful — than any drug I'd ever taken."

Ward's engaging smile dropped suddenly and his demeanor became serious.

"I kept going back, and she never realized I wasn't like her. She never knew I wasn't a good Christian boy. And the more I got to know her, the more that bothered me. I hated lying to her, and I began to resent what I was. But when I wasn't with her, my friends would suck me right back into that life she didn't know about. And the deeper into drugs I got, the more I wanted to be what she thought I was, the more I wanted to be free. But the worse I felt about myself, the worse my drug habit became. It all just spiraled out of control until I ruined everything."

He shook his head. "The last time I saw her, she was crying, because of me, because she'd finally discovered the real me, and the real me couldn't be the person she needed."

A frown line formed on his forehead between his dark eyebrows as he shook his head sadly. "She was the best thing that ever happened to me and I destroyed her because of who I was . . . because of what I smoked."

Gulping back the sudden desire to cry, Ansley reached out and touched his cheek on her screen.

When he lifted his face as soon as she made contact, as if he felt her touch, she jerked her hand back with a gasp.

"That's what happens when you do drugs," he said, addressing the students in the video with him. "Everyone you truly care about pays because of what you do. You might think you're only doing it to yourself. But you're not. They will get hurt because of you, and in the end, you'll lose them because that's the only way you can protect them."

Sniffing, Ansley wiped at her cheeks, glad to find them dry. But her eyes still burned for even the hint of moisture.

She didn't need to listen to any more; she knew what she was going to do. She had to see him again. She could tell herself it was only because she wanted seventeen years' worth of answers or maybe because she wanted to put her silly, youthful infatuation to rest and continue with her life. But the truth was, she simply ached to see him.

After copying his email address off his Danny's Haven page, she exited the website and logged into her email host, only to find a letter from him already sitting in her in-box, waiting for her to read.

CHAPTER FIVE

The ruckus outside his opened office door drew Ward from his pile of paperwork he was having no luck concentrating on. He pushed from his chair and hurried into the commons area to find Desi wiggling in between two yelling boys.

The teens' faces darkened to scarlet anger as they shouted accusations at the top of their lungs.

Trying desperately to stop them, Desi set a hand on each of their chests, manually shoving them apart. But at five feet, two inches tall, she looked painfully inept at her task, especially since she stood between two boys edging close to six feet.

"Hey!" Ward shouted, rushing forward. Reinforcing Desi's efforts, he stepped between the two boys as well. "What's going on here?"

"Little tattletale here is trying to rat me out for something I ain't even done." A kid named Zack reached past Ward to jab a condemning finger at the accused tattletale.

"I'm telling you, he's got crack on him." Trevor, a fifteen-year-old high school dropout, gritted his teeth as he glared back at Zack. "He just tried to sell me a rock."

As Desi took Trevor's arm and backed him ten feet away from Zack, Ward turned to the possible dealer.

"You carrying?" he asked in a low, serious voice.

Zack threw up his hands, glaring. "No way, man. He's lying."

"I came here to get away from that stuff," Trevor yelled past Desi's shoulder. "I don't want drugs shoved in my face when I'm trying to —"

Ward turned slowly to narrow a glare at Trevor. Instantly, the teen stopped his rant and shrank back. With an exhausted groan, Ward returned his attention to Zack. "I'm going to ask you one last time. Are you carrying?"

"No!"

"So, I won't find anything when I search you?"

When Zack's eyes flared and he lurched a step back, Ward countered by looming a step forward and catching him by the front of his shirt.

"I don't have anything on me," the boy insisted, even though the panic gathering on his face said otherwise.

He grappled with Ward, trying to shrug him off, which only angered Ward into gripping his arm and patting the outside of the kid's jeans pockets. Instantly, he heard the crinkle of plastic and felt hard pebbles inside.

"It's not what you think," Zack cried desperately. "It's not —"

"Take them out," Ward growled.

Zack cast a leery glance at Ward's face and scurried to obey. With shaking hands, he yanked the plastic bag full of drugs from his pocket and handed them over.

Ward fisted his fingers around the bag and pointed toward the exit. "Now get out."

Eyes flaring with fear, Zack gulped. "But —"

"Out!" Ward roared.

Silence echoed throughout the crowded commons room. Uninvolved kids shrank into the couches and chairs where they sat. Ward's arm felt like stone as he continued to point at the exit. Zack's face glazed with shame before he hung his head and slumped away. Just as he opened the door, Ward called, "And don't come back until you're ready to clean up your act."

Zack didn't answer, but he paused a moment before he dragged his feet into the darkening evening.

No one moved seconds after he left. Ward glanced around him to find every teen, and Desi too, gaping at him as if he'd lost his mind.

"What?" he demanded.

Trevor shook his head. "Dude, I've never seen you throw anyone out before."

Well, there was a first time for everything. Ward shrugged as if it was no big deal. "He brought drugs in."

"Yeah but —"

Okay, so this wasn't the first time anyone had snuck drugs into the center and been caught doing it. And no, Ward hadn't told any of those offenders to leave. But he had seen Care toss plenty of kids out over the years. Heck, he'd seen Desi expel her fair share.

Usually, he liked to take offenders into his office, talk to them, and eventually let them off with a minor slap on the hand. But today, he wasn't in the mood. He was too nervous, waiting for some kind of response from Ansley.

It'd been twenty-two hours since he'd accidently sent her that email. And he was going insane already, as well as becoming increasingly annoyed by a dozen kids gaping at him as if he'd just pulled out a gun and pointed it at their heads.

"He lied to me," he cried, defending himself. "I'm not in the mood to be lied to today, all right?"

A couple girls shrank back. He grunted out his frustrations and spun away to head to his office.

"Yo, Ward!" Desi's call caught him just as he hit the doorway.

He clenched his teeth, in no disposition to get a lecture from a co-worker either, but he ground to a halt. Slowly easing around, he lifted one eyebrow as she bounded forward.

Around them, the teens slowly began talking again in low, hushed voices, easing back into what they'd been doing before the fight had broken out and disrupted their comfort zone.

Easing his gaze from them, he focused on Desi and silently held the confiscated drugs for her to dispose of.

Meeting him in the doorway, she snatched the baggie from his hand, balled her fingers around it and pressing her fist against her hip as she eyed him up and down.

"You okay, bud?" she finally asked in a low voice, keeping their conversation somewhat confidential.

He nodded though his neck prickled with deceit as he did so. "Sure. Why?"

She shrugged. "Don't know. You've just been wiggy all day, not really yourself, not since that last presentation we gave. Are the testimonials finally getting to you or what?"

He shook his head. "Na. I'm fine. Really," he added when she merely narrowed her eyes.

Desi snorted. "Yeah, I'm not buying it."

Blowing out a heavy breath, Ward closed his eyes and rubbed his face. He'd already confided in Care. He didn't really want to spill his problems to anyone else. But behind her gruff façade, Desi looked honestly concerned.

"Look, I have a personal problem —"

Her gasp cut him off. He opened his eyes to find her attention not on him but across the room. Her mouth fell open as she gawked at something over his shoulder. "Whoa," she uttered, her gaze wide and dazed.

Figuring Zack had returned, he began to whirl around to kick some serious butt, but Desi caught his arm, stopping him.

"I saw her first," she hissed.

He blinked, taken aback. A moment later, he noticed her dazed gaze looked interested not upset.

Realizing it must be a pretty woman who'd just entered the center, he snorted and rolled his eyes. "Oh, please. Like I'd ever fight you over a woman. Besides, what're the odds she plays for your team, anyway?"

Scowling at him for that response, Desi shoved him lightly in the chest. "Hey, a girl can dream, can't she? And I want to dream about her."

Needing to see what had gotten Desi into such a tizzy, he glanced over his shoulder, grinning as he searched for a beautiful woman. Spotting her almost immediately, he froze. The smile fled his lips, the color drained from his face, and whatever he'd been about to say deserted his tongue.

It was her.

He hadn't seen her in seventeen years, but he knew immediately. She had bloomed from adorable teen into a striking woman.

Ansley.

The name wavered through him with a jerky kind of anxious dance like a hyper butterfly, fluttering without destination and too wired on sweet nectar to care about direction.

"Oh God," he whispered. Even as his heart leapt — yeah, leapt — a dreaded chill covered him, icing his arms and freezing a portion of his brain, making it incapable for him to think rationally.

He reeled back to Desi, his eyes so large he thought she should look magnified as he gaped at her. But instead, she appeared far away, even though he knew he could reach out and grasp her arm to steady himself, which is exactly what he did. He feared his feet were no longer capable of supporting him.

"What-do-I-do?" he rushed the question, nearly squeezing her arms off and almost tempted to shake an immediate answer out of her.

"Uh . . ." Desi blinked, looking utterly boggled. She glanced over his shoulder at Ansley, then returned her gaze to him. "I take it you know her."

He swallowed. Had he ever really known Ansley Marlow? He'd done nothing but lie to her from the very beginning of their acquaintance. But a split second later, he decided, yes, he'd known her. She might've been clueless as to who and what he really was, but he'd known her better than he'd ever known anyone. Even himself.

He nodded. "I . . . I got her pregnant when she was fifteen," he blurted out the explanation, having no clue why he decided to spill that little information bomb.

As Desi's mouth dropped open, he quickly explained, "I didn't know I had a daughter until we did our presentation at J. Edgar and she approached me after you and Care had already left."

Yeah, okay, that was technically the truth. He'd known a child had been created, but from that point on, he'd been in the dark, not sure if Ansley's parents had let her keep the baby, if she'd had a miscarriage, or even if it had been a boy or a girl. But he didn't have time to go into the details, plus it made him look less like a loser to insinuate he hadn't known anything about Brooklyn all these years.

Desi's eyes widened to the size of walnuts. Her gaping mouth moved, but no words came out. Suddenly, she shifted a look over his shoulder and puffed out a gasp. "Quick. She's coming this way."

Cold sweat dribbled down the center of his back. "I can't talk to her like this," he confessed on barely a whisper. Not now. He wasn't prepared, though what he would've done to prepare, he had no idea. With enough warning, he probably would've panicked himself into an early grave.

"I'll get rid of her," Desi immediately assured him, making him want to hug her for having his back. Her blind trust warmed him. The friends he kept these days were a trillion times better than the "friends" he'd hung around when he was eighteen.

But from across the room, a teen shoved open the door to the gym and shouted, "Hey, Ward!" at the top of his lungs. "Wanna shoot some hoops?"

Ward flinched, thinking he could strangle Jace Buchannan. The seventeen-year-old was one of their newest teens. Ward had been spending a little more personal time with him than usual because the boy reminded him so much of himself at that age. He was a good kid with a good heart, but he came from the worst kind of family.

Risking a glance across the room, Ward watched Jace flash him a genuine grin as he tossed a basketball back and forth between his hands. Obviously having missed the big show of Ward throwing Zack out of the clinic, Jace wore shorts and a thin, holey shirt. He looked ready to spend a hearty, sweaty hour of beating Ward at a game of horse.

His face still feeling as white as paste, Ward shook his head tightly. "Not . . . not today, bud." Unable to control his neck, he glanced toward the last place he'd seen her.

Ansley.

She was already closer, moving past the couches in the center of the large room where half a dozen teens had gathered in front of a television, setting up a movie to watch. And her gaze was locked on him. Target spotted, missiles engaged, she headed in for the kill. He tried to swallow but found he couldn't gulp past the knot that had formed in his gullet. Trapped in her gaze, he stared back.

"Busted." Desi patted his arm. "Guess I won't get rid of her for you after all. Sorry, bud."

The small woman slipped away after giving him a supportive pat on the arm, and she disappeared before Ward could reach out and drag her back to him. He needed all the support he could get right now. But Desi moved too fast for him to catch.

He swallowed and returned his attention to Ansley as she stopped in front of him.

Five feet separated them, but it felt more like inches. She was so close. This had to be a dream.

When she didn't speak, just stood there, he drew in a breath. "Ansley?"

She nodded, a quick, efficient bob of the head. "You . . . you gave me this address as your work contact."

He had? Why, oh why had he done that?

He didn't want her here, had hoped if she responded to him at all, it would be through email where he wouldn't have to hear her voice or see her face. Smell her skin.

She was so beautiful. Stunning.

He couldn't concentrate.

He'd played her up in his mind so much through the years, he'd been so sure she couldn't be as pretty as he thought he remembered.

And she wasn't. She was better. So much better.

Looking at her physically hurt him. It made him regret and wish for things he knew he could never have.

No do-overs, he reminded himself. He had to make the best of what he had to work with now.

"Why don't we . . ." he started only to realize inviting her into his office, alone, might be inappropriate. Would it scare her? Clearing his throat, he ducked his head. But where were they supposed to talk if they didn't find some privacy? He didn't figure she wanted their past discussed out here in the open any more than he did.

"Do you want to step into my office?" he finally just asked.

He lifted his face to catch her answer. She nodded her compliance and he nearly passed out.

She did?

That had to be promising if she didn't outright object to the idea of being alone with him. She didn't even look apprehensive about it.

Swallowing, he shuffled backward into his cluttered lair, letting her follow. "Sorry about the mess. I'm not too . . . organized."

When she shut the door behind her, trapping them inside alone, he gawked, doubly surprised. He'd been planning on keeping the door open, or at least cracked, so she wouldn't feel any angst.

But he had the strangest sensation the only one worried about their closeted proximity was him.

"So, uh . . ." He scrubbed his hands on his thighs and let out a nervous chuckle. "Someone really ought to write the manual of proper procedure for this kind of conversation. I don't know what to say. Do we talk about the weather first, or what?"

She sent him a small, uneasy smile of amusement. "It's getting cold out there."

He nodded. "Yeah."

She blew out a breath. Ward cleared his throat.

The silence that followed nearly made him stroke out. It bothered him more than avoiding the topic they were both there to discuss. Unable to handle it a moment longer, he burst out. "Okay, I have a million and one questions to ask about her but for the life of me, I can't think up one."

She began to wring her hands. "You want to know about Brooklyn?"

Why did she look so worried? He rubbed his numb face. "Yeah, I . . . Well, the biggest questions have already been answered, I guess. You had the baby, obviously. You kept her, and she was a girl. Her name is Brooklyn and she's sixteen, attending J. Edgar Hoover High School. And . . . and she looked healthy when I saw her."

Licking her lips, Ansley nodded uneasily. "She is."

Ward nodded as well. "Good. She seemed . . . fairly intelligent."

"Straight A's." Pride lined Ansley's face.

His eyebrows arched with surprise. "Really?" He blew out an impressed, intimidated breath. "Wow." His kid was a genius and the best grade he'd ever gotten in school was a C plus.

Ansley shifted, drawing his attention to her legs. In her straight knee-length business skirt, they looked so lovely with such feminine, shapely calves and slim ankles. Her pumps bore a low heel and his gaze fell to them for some odd reason.

The woman was flawless from head to toe.

Realizing he was ogling her shoes of all things, he zipped his gaze up to find her glancing longingly at a visitor's chair wedged in front of his desk.

"I'm sorry. Do you want to sit down?" he asked belatedly.

She sent him an uneasy smile and eased into the seat. He pulled his own chair out from behind his desk and rolled it around the side but made sure to keep plenty of distance between them. As soon as he lowered himself, however, the door to his office burst open.

Care appeared, her hair scattered and chest heaving out of breath as if she'd sprinted. "I just heard — Desi told me —" Her wide eyes had been on him until she focused on the woman seated in front of his desk. She jerked to a halt and stared at Ansley before gulping and easing into the room, silently clicking the door shut behind her.

As still air echoed around them with an eerie, unnatural quiet, Ward lurched to his feet. Pointing out Care, he introduced, "This is my boss, Caren Boyer. Care, this is . . . Ansley."

The two women nodded to each other.

Ansley remained seated, her hands pressed firmly in her lap. Care hovered by the door, gawking badly. Ward wanted to smack her in the shoulder and tell her to stop. But about as soon as he wondered if he should nudge some sense back into her, Care seemed to regain her sanity. She colored and sent him an apologetic smile.

"Excuse me for interrupting," she said, turning back to Ansley and instantly facing him again. "But Desi, uh, informed me who was here and I thought — realized really — that your forthcoming conversation might become a bit tense or overly emotional, so I decided to offer my, uh, service as a third-party mediator if either of you would feel more comfortable with someone else in the room."

Ward's shoulders slumped. Instant relief washed over him. With Care here, she could ease any nerves that might attack Ansley. But when he glanced Ansley's way, he found her eyes wide and glazed with shock, her face drained of color.

Concern knit his brow. "Do you want her to stay?"

She began to shake her head forcefully before she stopped herself, then offered Care a tight smile. "N-no. No thank you."

Yeesh. Ward's stomach plummeted into

his knees. He'd been counting on Care to help him through this.

"We're good." His voice rasped as he supported Ansley's decision.

Care paused to sear him with a look, her gaze unreadable, but he could feel her worry and concern. He nodded to let her know he'd be fine, though his nod was a whole heck of a lot more confident than the anxiety prowling through his abdomen.

She opened the door, disappeared from the room, and quietly closed it behind her.

Left alone with him once again, Ansley let out an audible breath and whirled around. "How much does she know?" Her voice sounded small and devastated. She looked horrified.

He swallowed, pretty sure she wouldn't like his answer, but he stuck with the truth. "Everything."

She didn't react, and he longed to know what she thought.

Hands as cold as ice, he rubbed them along his thighs. "If it'd make you more comfortable, I can call her back."

But she shook her head avidly. "No," she rushed out the word. "No this will be awkward enough with just the two of us. A stranger present wouldn't help me at all."

"Okay. That's fine. No problem." He

slowly eased back into his chair. "So . . ." he said, not sure where to go from there.

She didn't appear to have any clue about what to say either.

Could he ask her how she was? She looked well, physically fit with all her limbs and sanity intact. She looked better than good actually. But he darted his gaze away because he didn't want to be caught ogling again, didn't want to her to know how much he wanted to devour her with his stare.

He'd thought of her so much through the years, prayed for a time machine so he could go back and replay everything again.

"How long have you worked here?" she asked, making him jump and dart his attention to her, catching how she gazed around his jumbled office and took in all the photos and notes posted to his crowded walls.

"Oh." He blew out a breath, trying to think. Dear Lord, if she asked him his name, he doubted he'd be able to answer that either. "It's been, uh, about . . . seven years, I think." He squinted, remembering before he nodded. "Yeah. It'll be eight years in January. So, seven . . . seven and a half years."

She bobbed her head, drew in a breath, then asked, "How long have you been . . . been . . . ?"

He arched a brow and filled in the blank. "Clean?"

She flushed and nodded again, but her dark eyes focused on him so intently, he felt singled out, chosen. His chest tightened with achy pressure. He cleared his throat. "I've been off drugs without a relapse for eleven years."

She shuddered out a breath and her eyes filled with an achy kind of agony. Her voice hoarse, she asked, "And why didn't you ever come back?"

If she'd taken out a crowbar and walloped him in the chest, he couldn't have been more surprised. She actually looked upset that he'd never returned to her life. Vision spotting in and out, he struggled for breath before managing to respond. "You . . . you actually wanted me to?"

She looked down at her hands that she'd twisted together before quietly admitting, "I don't know."

He eased back in his seat, trying to beat down the hope rising in his chest.

When she lifted her face, he held his breath for what she might say next. "In your email, you made it sound like you wanted to be a part of Brooklyn's life."

He nodded silently, unable to verbalize such a deep desire out loud.

"Then why are you making this decision now? What's changed in the past eleven years since you've been clean to do this now?"

He deflated, looked down at his hands, and frowned. "I . . . I guess it was because of something Brooklyn said to me that made me think she wants to know me, despite what I was."

Ansley leaned forward in her chair, looking intent. "What did she say?"

He cleared his throat. "She said she wanted to volunteer at Danny's Haven because of her father. She knew what he — what I — used to be, and she wanted to feel like maybe she had helped me if she did something to help others like me."

Covering her mouth, Ansley stared at him from wide brown eyes.

His hands began to shake and his voice wavered. "I just . . . it really resonated with me, even before I knew who she was. And I didn't want her to feel lacking in any way because of the mistakes I'd made." He laughed at himself softly. "I don't know what I'm thinking. I'm sure she's too old to need anything to do with me now. I know I couldn't possibly make up for years of absence or for what I did to you but . . ." He closed his eyes. When he opened them, he lifted his face to look to Ansley for guidance. "What do you think?" he whispered.

She licked her lips, looking indecisive. "I don't know," she whispered back. "It's been such a long time."

He nodded. "Yeah."

When she nibbled at the corner of her lips, he almost broke down and wept. He hadn't thought he'd ever get to see her do that again.

She straightened her back and smoothed her hands across her lap, straightening wrinkles in her skirt that hadn't been there. "I suppose your goal is to gain some kind of custody over her."

"I . . ." Ward stared at her blankly. The word custody had never even entered his brain. No wonder why she'd looked nervous earlier. "No," he said, only to flush. "I mean, I don't know what my goal is exactly. Just to . . . to meet her, I guess. I want her to know who I am. I want to know who she is. And if she wants to hang out or something after that, that would be great."

Ansley scrutinized him a moment before slowly repeating, "Hang out?"

"You know." He flailed his hand in a useless gesture. "I'm sure she's too old for sleepovers and alternating every other weekend and stuff like that. Besides, I don't have a spare bedroom. She'd have to sleep on the couch. Er, I mean, I could take the couch, no problem. But I'm not a very good cook and I don't have very nutritious food in the house. Though, yeah, I could go grocery shopping and . . ." When he realized he was rambling, badly, he groaned and sank his face into his hands. "I'm messing this up, aren't I?"

"No," she said in a reassuring voice that made him pop up in surprise. She offered him a soft smile. "You're saying you just want to meet her and go from there."

"Yeah." He smiled back, remembering when he used to try to tell her things back when they'd first known each other. He'd always butcher his explanations, yet she still figured out what he was really trying to say.

"Well." Blowing out a breath, she pushed to her feet. "I'll think about it and let you know what I decide."

His grin dropped flat. "Oh." Scrambling to recover his scattered wits, he shot to his feet and nodded vigorous. "Yeah," he said. "Okay. Yeah, definitely let me know."

Except, why didn't she know right now what she wanted? What possible reason would she have for not knowing now? Either she wanted their daughter to know him, or she didn't. Right?

It hurt. But he understood. Totally.

This wasn't a decision she could take lightly, because seriously, why would any sane woman trust her daughter around him for any length of time? He should feel relieved she hadn't given him an immediate no.

But he didn't feel relieved.

Working through the disappointment, he forced a weak smile. "You know where to find me."

As she walked out the door, all the warmth and vitality in the room fled with her. He sank into his chair, lost and drained. What was he supposed to do now?

CHAPTER SIX

"I'll think about it," Ansley repeated the words she kept telling everyone these days as she paused in front of the opened mirror of her medicine cabinet and rubbed at her throbbing temples. She sighed when she spotted her bottle full of pills, telling herself she didn't need them.

Her migraines weren't as severe as some people she'd heard of having. She didn't grow physically ill to the point of vomiting. Her vision never left her. But a light layer of sweat blanketed her, and her muscles cramped as her pulse surged through her ears.

Fingers shaking, she reached for the bottle.

Since learning about Ward's true lifestyle seventeen years ago, she'd grown leery of taking any kind of prescription, afraid of becoming as addicted as he had. She used her pills sparingly. But with all the stress and drama plaguing her lately, her head felt like it was going to twist off and roll across the floor, and her entire body ached.

She popped a single tablet into her mouth and quickly screwed the cap back on, putting the bottle away. After she washed the bitter taste down with a glass of water and closed the cabinet door, she stared at her reflection in the mirror, taking in the deep purple smudges of exhaustion underlining her eyes.

"I'll think about it," she repeated. But she didn't want to think about anything. Not Preston's proposal, not Brooklyn's wish to volunteer at a dangerous clinic, and not Ward's request to meet his daughter.

"Yeah, I'll think about it," she muttered, feeling like a coward. She already knew what she wanted to do in each case, so why was she stalling?

Maybe because she knew no one would approve of what she really wanted, maybe because a part of her didn't approve either, realizing she wanted to act on silly emotions rather than solid logic and good outside advice.

When her doorbell gonged, her nerves wrenched painfully, making her whimper as she jumped at the sound.

This couldn't be good. In the past two

days, she nearly shot through the roof every time the phone or doorbell rang, which had only been twice today, thank goodness. Both had been more calls from Kelsey. Brooklyn had finally gone over to her friend's house at noon, leaving Ansley alone to think.

Lord, she was so tired of thinking.

Hurrying from the bathroom, she raced through the house and checked the peek hole. She wasn't sure what she'd do if it was Ward. Her heart raced at the mere thought of possibly seeing him again, but who could tell if the racing came from excitement or dread.

It wasn't Ward.

It was Preston.

She groaned and closed her eyes before pulling the door open.

"Hey there." Sweeping over the threshold, he entered the living room to give her a brief hug and peck on the cheek. "I tried your cell phone, but it went straight to voice mail."

"Oh. Yeah." Ansley winced when pain shot through her temples. "I'm sorry. I turned it off. I've had a pounding headache all day."

His face crinkled with worry as his hand went to her brow. "Another migraine?"

"Yes," she grumbled. "I thought I was finally getting over these things. It's been a few months since I last had one."

"Well, cranial complications don't heal overnight." His rational, doctor's voice kind of irritated her, making the twinge in her temples sharper. "Did you take one of your pills?"

She nodded. "I just did. Thank goodness it's Saturday though. I don't think I would've been able to make it through a day of work in this condition."

"Come on." Face crinkling with pity, he took her shoulders and led her deeper into the house. "I'll make you some hot tea."

After he sat her in a kitchen chair, he pulled open the exact cupboard holding her kettle. Amazed he'd learned his way around her kitchen in the eight months they'd been casually dating, she watched him pull out two cups and dig up a couple tea bags. All the while, he told her about his week, slipping in amusing little tidbits about things his patients had said and done.

When he finally had them both a steaming mug full of chamomile, he sat across from her and took a sip when she did.

For his mid-forties, he was still attractive. Preston had a slim build, with a long, slim face and hollowed cheeks dipping in between a long, slim nose. His glasses gave him an astute appeal and framed a lovely set of soft brown eyes. But never would he hold a candle to the rugged dark-haired, blue-eyed enigma of Ward Gemmell.

Closing her eyes, Ansley told herself to stop comparing and forced her brain to focus on the way the steam helped clear her head. The pills were beginning to work as well, easing the ache.

"So?" Preston said, sounding expectant.

She blinked her eyes open. Preston watched her, waiting.

"So . . . what?" she asked dumbly.

He frowned. "So, did you talk to Brooklyn? What did she think?"

"Talk to Brooklyn about what?" Her lashes fluttered with confusion as Ansley rubbed at her brow.

Preston stared at her a moment before he broke out laughing. "Don't tease." He slapped a playful hand her way. "Did she oppose the idea of us getting married or not?"

Freezing motionless, Ansley gaped at him. "I . . . I'm so sorry, Preston. I've been terribly scrambled since she told me about —" When it struck her that he had no idea what she'd been going through, she slapped her forehead, which didn't help her headache in the least. "I haven't even talked to her about it yet."

His grin died. "You haven't? Why not?"

Heat suffused her cheeks. "I . . ." Her mouth hung open as she tried to figure out how to tell him about Ward. When she spotted her closed laptop sitting on the center of the table, she reached for it. "Here. Maybe you should just read the email."

Preston blinked, looking utterly confused. "Email?"

She nodded. "Just . . ." after clicking her way into her mail, she opened Ward's message and turned the screen to face him. "Read this. It should explain everything."

He did.

"So?" She chewed on the corner of her bottom lip as she watched him reread Ward's letter. "What do you think?"

He lifted his face, his eyebrows rising above the rims of his glasses. "Think? I think you should trash this preposterous letter. Now. Before Brooklyn accidentally stumbles across it." He motioned toward the screen with one finger, contorting his features into disgust. "He said he'd respect any decision you made and would stay out of her life if you didn't contact him. So just don't contact him, and hopefully this will go away."

She blinked, not expecting that kind of advice at all. It just didn't seem . . . responsible. "But —"

"If you think he's lying and will try to talk to her without your permission, I have a lawyer on retainer who could probably scare him off and keep him away for good. I doubt we'll even need to pay him —"

"Pay him?" Ansley stared at Preston as if she'd never seen him before, when in fact, she wondered if she had — really seen him, that is. For some reason, she couldn't tell him she'd already approached Ward. She didn't want to tell him because she knew he'd chastise her. "So you don't think I should tell Brooklyn about him at all then?"

He sent her a startled glance. "Why in heaven's name would you tell her? You haven't told her anything about him so far. Not even his name. What's changed?"

Everything!

She sputtered. "Well . . . I . . . He . . . he's been absent from her life all these years. I didn't want to give her any kind of false hope."

"Exactly. So why change that now?"

"Because he's no longer absent. She's met him. He's met her. Granted, she didn't know who he was. But he knows who she is, plus he's contacted me about it. I . . . it just feels wrong to ignore this as if it never happened."

"Honey." Preston's tone turned placating as he took her hands in his and tightened his grip. "This . . . person abandoned you in your biggest time of need and has been absent from Brooklyn's life since before she was born. You do not owe him anything."

"But what about Brooklyn?" she had to ask. "Don't I owe her a father?"

He flinched, pain flashing briefly across his features. After opening his mouth to talk, he paused. She could see him thinking his next words through, tactfully putting them together before he said, "I had hoped I . . . could be a father to her."

Ansley's eyes widened. Wrapping her fingers around his, she instantly started to gush. "I'm so sorry, Preston. I didn't mean to exclude you from anything. I just . . ." She shook her head, not wanting to hurt him further. "No, you're right," she confirmed. "You've been more of a parent to her than he ever has. It was silly of me to think blood ties meant anything when he's shown me through his absence it obviously means nothing to him. I just wish . . ."

She pictured Ward's face on that video when he'd talked about her. He'd been so open about his faults, and he'd looked so repentant. It made her want . . . she shamefully wanted what she had wanted seventeen years ago. She wanted him, her, and their baby to make a family together.

But what was she thinking? That was impossible. It was absurd to even crave it. She would never be able to trust Ward Gemmell, even if he did appear to be completely changed. The man had abandoned her in her biggest time of need, after all.

"You just wish what?" Preston asked earnestly, stroking his thumb over her knuckles.

She jerked her gaze to him. Something inside her began to burn, scalding hotter with each second she studied him. When she realized it was guilt, she glanced away.

Why, oh, why couldn't she look at him and feel the same tingling thrill she'd felt yesterday in Ward's office? Why did she want to pull her hand away from Preston when she'd wanted to reach out and simply touch Ward?

"I wish he'd never run into Brooklyn," she grated out the words, cringing because it was a lie and biting her lip because she knew it's what she really should want.

She should hate him. He'd transformed her from an obedient, good Christian girl into an unwed teenage mother. He'd abandoned her and broken her heart. He'd done nothing but lie to her when they had known each other. So why did she keep dreaming about that boy she'd met during her Bible study group? That boy didn't exist — had never existed — and she should by no means seek him from the man wanting to meet her daughter.

"I'll have my lawyer contact him," Preston said with a note of finality in his voice as he patted her hand and drew his fingers away.

"No!" she cried, reaching out to clutch him. "Please. This is my problem. I'll deal with it."

His gaze frosted with outrage. "But —"

"It's okay," she assured him, her voice soothing even though her pulse jerked with panic. The last thing she wanted was for Preston — or worse, his lawyer — to get involved.

"But I want to protect you, Ansley."

And there was another reason she was so hesitant to marry him. His protection felt too constricting, too much like how her parents had treated her after she'd gotten mixed up with Ward. Domineering, smothering. Life-sucking. They had suddenly started forbidding her to do things she'd always freely done before, swearing it was for her own good. She'd begun sneaking out when the idea wouldn't have crossed her mind a year earlier.

One time, when she'd been four months pregnant, she'd climbed out her window just to watch a movie at the theatre by herself. She'd had to fight tooth and nail to move away from home — when she was twenty-one — because her parents were so worried about her raising Brooklyn by herself.

Now, at thirty-two, she certainly didn't want to marry another parental authority. She wanted a husband.

"I'll be fine," she assured Preston. "Truly. Just . . . let me handle this my way."

His eyes narrowed as if he didn't trust her.

"She's my daughter," she bit out, annoyed. Why did everyone look over that fact?

Finally, he backed off. Lifting his hands, he settled back in his chair and studied her from across the table. "You're right. Just know I'll be here if you need me."

Great. Now she felt guilty all over again. All he wanted to do was help her. Rubbing at the dull ache in her temple, she closed her eyes. "I'm sorry. I didn't mean to snap. I appreciate the offer, but please, I'd like to deal with this my way first."

He nodded but said nothing.

She offered him a tremulous smile. "What say we go out for dinner? Brooklyn's at a friend's and I haven't eaten much today.

My migraine is abating already, which always leaves me famished."

With a genial smile, Preston pushed to his feet. "Sounds great. I'm craving Mexican. What about you?"

Relieved they had moved past Ward, Ansley nodded. "Sounds good to me."

As he helped her clear the tea cups from the table and clean up the kitchen, she glanced protectively toward her laptop, glad he hadn't pressed her to delete the email, because she didn't think she would've been able to. She simply could not erase Ward from her hard drive . . . or her heart.

CHAPTER SEVEN

Ward rapped his knuckles against Care's partially opened office door and stuck his head through the crack to find Jace inside with her. "Hey. You wanted to see me?"

She waved him forward. "Yes. Please come in, Ward."

He frowned slightly, wondering what was wrong, and cast a sideways glance at Jace, who refused to look at him as he wrung his hands in his lap.

Shutting the door behind him, Ward entered and slid into the seat next to the teen. "What's up?"

Care cleared her throat, sent her own speculative glance toward Jace, and turned back to Ward. "We're having an intervention."

Ward paused. A what? He glanced at Jace, startled, and swerved back to Care. "For who?"

An almost amused expression flittered

across Care's features before she averted her gaze. "For you."

"Me?" He straightened, then laughed. "What? Why?"

Care definitely wouldn't look him in the eye now. "Some people at Danny's Haven have grown concerned about your . . . recent behavior."

"My . . ." Ward whirled toward Jace. "Because I didn't play basketball with you the other evening?" he asked, incredulous.

"Dude, it's not just that," the boy immediately began. "You've been weird all week. And I heard about what you did to Zack. Something's up with you. And you always say a person can tell when someone falls off the wagon. They start acting strange and —"

"Wait, wait, wait," Ward butted in, waving his hands. "You think I've fallen off the wagon?" He let out another laugh and turned toward Care.

She offered no assistance, only shrugged with a rueful expression.

Shaking his head, stupefied by the entire encounter, Ward whirled back to Jace. "Bud, trust me. I haven't turned back to drugs."

The teen merely lifted a skeptical brow. "Like you'd really own up to it if you had."

Ward threw back his head and barked out

an unbelieving laugh. "Are you serious? You really think . . ." His words died off when he saw the expression on Jace's face. The kid was honestly worried about him. Shaking his head, he lifted his hands in surrender. "Okay, this is getting ridiculous. I haven't fallen off the wagon. I haven't started taking drugs again. I have . . . personal issues going on, okay, and —"

"You said personal issues will cause a person to decline and revert to toking it up, just to take off the edge," Jace reminded him.

Ward nearly growled at him. "I know what I said, but . . ." Fed up with the third degree, he glanced at Care for support. "Why are you allowing this? You actually know what I'm going through."

She nodded in a stern professional manner, freaking him out with her placid poker face. "Yes, I do know what kind of personal issues you're dealing with, but it's affecting your work, Ward." She motioned to the teen next to him. "Jace has noticed a change in you, as I'm sure every other kid in the program has."

Ward's mouth dropped open as he gaped at her, unable to believe what he was hearing. Was she accusing him of neglecting his work? Scaring the kids? What?

"I . . . I'm not sure what you expect me to do? I can't help what's been happening. But I can promise you I haven't turned to drugs because of it. Do you want me to take a test to prove I'm clean? Because I will if that's what you want."

"I do," Jace mumbled, raising his hand a moment before meekly lowering it.

Ward glanced at him sharply and turned back to Care. For the life of him, he couldn't tell what was going on inside her head.

But she didn't tell him not to take the test.

He shrugged as if it made no difference, but deep down, he felt shattered. "Fine," he muttered.

He'd always assumed she trusted him more than this. For seven years, he'd thought of Caren Boyer as a mother figure, as a mentor and a friend, someone he could trust. And if she couldn't trust him back —

"Good." Jace sounded satisfied. He sprang to his feet, smiling with a relieved glow. "I guess that's settled then." Dusting his hands off onto his thighs as if he'd just accomplished a dirty task, he started for the door. "Catch you guys later."

A full minute after Jace was gone, Ward remained seated, silent and pensive. The very foundation he'd worked all these years to build for himself after straightening up his life had been rocked. One of his closest friends, boss or not, thought he'd slipped, thought he'd returned to his former self.

"You need to deal with this," she said, her voice more irritated than soothing.

He sliced her a defiant glance, wanting to hiss something bitter and sarcastic. Thanks for having my back, or something like that. But he was still too shattered to think up a good comeback.

"I thought I was," he growled instead.

"Well, you're doing a sucky job at it."

He gaped, even more astounded by her anger. At him! "And how exactly do you expect me to act?"

Her eyebrow arched. "Maybe with a little maturity."

Ward didn't know how he could get any more shocked than he'd been since discovering he'd been pulled into an intervention, or that maybe his best friend on earth had no faith in him, but this blew his mind.

"Maturity?" he repeated, trying to keep his voice level. "I have been as . . . as diplomatic as I can possibly be, Care. Everything I've done and said since meeting my daughter has been thoroughly thought through with consideration for Ansley's feelings. I —"

"And what about Brooklyn's feelings?" she

114

demanded.

Ward froze a moment, stumped, before he shook his head, not comprehending. "What do you mean?"

"My God, you have a child, Ward. It's time to take responsibility for her. You've been so busy tiptoeing around the mother, trying not to offend her, you haven't even considered Brooklyn in this. All the while, she keeps going through each day without her father."

"Again . . ." His voice lifted a notch. "What exactly do you think I should be doing that I'm not? I told Ansley I want to be a part of Brooklyn's life. Isn't the next step kind of up to her?"

"The first step should've been contacting a lawyer to get the time with Brooklyn you deserve."

"With my record?" he asked, unconvinced. "You think any judge in the country would let me near her if they saw my criminal past?" Besides he'd rather have Ansley's complete cooperation and acceptance than force her to give up parts of her daughter through legal means. He wanted this done amicably. It was the least he could do for the woman he'd left to raise his only child.

Plus he couldn't stomach the idea of doing anything else to make her hate him any more than she already must.

"I don't care what kind of bum you were when you were eighteen," Care nearly shouted. "I know you now, and the man I know would not ignore the fact he has a child out there."

"I'm not ignoring it," he said calmly, while inside he raged. What was Care trying to do to him? He was strung taut enough as it was, hoping he could meet Brooklyn as her father. "I want to know my child, okay. I want to send a check each month to support her. I want to be involved in her life. But this isn't my decision to make, and it's not your decision either. It's Ansley's. And if she thinks it is in Brooklyn's best interest for me to stay out of her life, I will fully respect that. I don't care how much it might kill me."

Sending him an irritated glower, Care folded her arms over her chest. "You're her biological father. You should have rights."

He rubbed at his face, groaning. "I can't talk about this right now. I can't . . . It's up to Ansley, and that's that. You don't have a say in the issue."

The killer glare she sent him told him how much she didn't appreciate his retort. But at the moment, he didn't care.

Pushing to his feet, he stormed from her office. As he blew into the hallway and entered the commons area, just about every kid in the place paused and looked up at him. He saw too many leery expressions to count.

Immediately, he took a breath so he could relax what must look like a feral expression. Despite how much it hurt to admit, Care had been right. This thing with Ansley was affecting his work. And these kids depended on him for their own peace of mind. He didn't want them to feel alienated in the least.

Giving himself no time to change his mind, Ward clapped his hands loudly. "Okay, everyone," he called. "Gather 'round the circle. It's time for another impromptu group session."

Plenty of groans ensued, accompanied with "but we're halfway through this movie," and "I'm about to break my record on this game." Ward merely strode to the center of the circle where they usually met for their group chats and set his hands firmly on his hips, waiting.

Slowly, teen after teen set their current activity aside and slunk toward the chairs.

"Who're we helping today?" Cory, the oldest of the group, asked as he fell heavily into a loveseat and tucked away a paddle he'd taken from the Ping-Pong table where he'd been playing a game with a new boy Ward hadn't met yet.

It was a common fact impromptu group sessions came about whenever one person had a big problem and needed extra support from the other teens in the center.

Instead of naming one of the teens however, Ward found Jace in the circle and made eye contact. He had approached his own chair but hadn't sat down yet.

Holding Jace's stare, Ward said, "Me. We're helping me."

"You?" came the incredulous reaction from everyone except Jace. Within two seconds, each chair in the circle was filled. Even Desi had appeared from her office with a curious expression and lingered around the outer fringes of the group.

"So, you are falling off the wagon then?" Jace asked gripping the seat of his chair, his eyes huge with worry.

Ward shook his head. "No."

"But —"

Holding up his hand, Ward waited until everyone quieted. Then he explained. "But I do have a problem, and it stems from my time as a user, so . . ." He shrugged. He wasn't sure if he could share this part of his life with them, but if he did, Care couldn't accuse him of slacking in his duties, not when he made his problems part of his job.

"Ward, dude," one of the veterans at the clinic named Aiden rolled his eyes. "I think everyone here has already heard your entire life story by now."

Realizing he might lose a lot of respect he'd spent the last seven years at Danny's Haven trying to accumulate, he glanced down at his hands. A piece of dried skin had begun to peel from a callous on his palm. He picked at it a moment before lifting his face. "You don't know everything."

The teens seated around him exchanged glances. Wishing he weren't standing in the middle of their circle, he took a deep breath and began. "I met a girl when I was using."

"Heard it," Cory called in a bored voice. "You were heavy into drugs. She was clean, and innocent, and knew nothing about your extracurricular activities. Chick was the love of your life, yada, yada, yada, and the last time you saw her, she was a watering pot, bawling all over the place."

Ward arched an unimpressed eyebrow. In return, Cory slouched farther in his seat, crossed his arms over his chest and sent him a smirk.

"So you already knew she was fifteen

when I met her then? And I was . . . eighteen."

Cory's smug smile froze. Ward watched the kid's eyes bug with realization. "So, that's like . . . statutory?"

"Exactly," Ward answered softly. He kept very still when the whispers started. Afraid to see condemnation from anyone in the circle, he kept his gaze focused on Cory, watching the kid's mouth fall open.

"Wait, wait, wait," Jace cut in, waving his hands. "You said your buddies called you Slammer because you always got caught for every illegal thing you did."

Ward closed his eyes. "That's right."

Silence answered him. When he lifted his lashes, he found every person in the room staring, their mouths slightly ajar.

Finally, Jace found his voice. "You did not go to jail for . . . for statutory rape."

After a single nod, Ward cleared his throat. "Three years."

"No way," Jace exploded. "No way. Just . . . that's not even possible. You? But you're the most harmless person I know."

Shrugging, Ward sent the boy a helpless look. His head was completely blank of what he should say next. He'd never ever planned on telling his kids anything about that part of his life. But as a challenge to Care, here he stood, blurting out everything.

"Why are you telling us this now?" Nudging Cory aside without even looking at the boy, Desi gazed at Ward with wide-eyed awe. "It happened a long time ago, why . . . ?" She shook her head, looking puzzled, until suddenly she gasped. "That woman who was here?"

Afraid his co-worker would never think of him the same again, Ward glanced away. "Yeah. When we went to J. Edgar Hoover High School last week, a girl approached me after you left with Care. She wanted to work here, to volunteer. After she left, I realized she was . . . my daughter."

Desi's mouth fell open.

"You have a daughter?" Jace exploded, incredulous.

"Okay, that I didn't know," Cory admitted.

A moment of silence followed before every person in the circle began to talk at once.

"Did you know?"

"How old is she?"

"What's her name?"

Ward lifted his hands to silence everyone, and they actually grew quiet, eager to listen to him.

"Yes," he admitted. "I knew she had been conceived, but I was in jail when she was born, so I didn't know she was girl. I didn't know her name, or even that her mother had decided to keep her. I don't even know what day she was born. When I was released, I didn't look them up to find out my answers because I thought the best thing I could do for them was stay away. I was pretty much a mess back then. So it was a total shock to meet my daughter the other day. She still doesn't know who I am, but the thing is, she said something to me that told me I needed to be a part of her life. And that's where we are today. I've spoken to her mother, and she said she'd think about letting me meet Brooklyn as her father. That's why I may seem a little irritable, or distressed, or distracted lately. I hope you please excuse my behavior. I'm waiting on the woman who sent me to jail for three years to give me permission to get to know her daughter."

CHAPTER EIGHT

When Ansley came through the back door of her house, her arms loaded with groceries, she could barely see over the top of the bag. But what she did see stopped her dead in her tracks.

Brooklyn sat frozen in front of Ansley's laptop she'd left out on the kitchen table. It was flipped up and open. With the teen's back to the doorway, Ansley couldn't see her daughter's expression. And she couldn't see the screen with Brooklyn's body blocking it.

Racking her brain, she tried to remember if she'd left Ward's email open or if she'd closed out of her account after showing it to Preston the day before. In either case, Brooklyn knew her password, but why would she go into Ansley's email for no reason? Except maybe to check and see if Ward had emailed her yet, which he'd told Brooklyn he would do.

"Honey, could you give me a hand with these groceries," she called, trying to sound nonchalant, as if her heart wasn't racing a million miles a minute. "I have more in the car."

Her daughter didn't immediately turn.

"Baby?" Ansley swallowed as she set her armload on the counter beside her. *Please, please, please,* she wished desperately, hoping Brooklyn hadn't gone into her emails. "You okay?"

The teen slowly swiveled, and Ansley could tell immediately. Brooklyn knew.

Her face stark white, and her eyes ringed red with tears, Brooklyn sniffed and wiped at her nose. "He's my father," she choked out the words.

Fumbling, Ansley hurried forward. "Brooklyn," she whispered, not sure what to say but ready to sooth her child in any way possible. "Please."

Eyes wide with distrust, Brooklyn scrambled from her chair and skipped backward. "I just wanted to see if he'd contacted you yet. I had no idea he was actually . . . Were you ever going to tell me?" she demanded, her voice shaky and hoarse.

"I . . . I . . ." Ansley shook her head. "I don't know. I was trying to decide what was best for you."

"Best for me?" Brooklyn cried. She pressed her hand against her heart, looking outraged. "You knew I wanted to meet him, to at least know his name. You've always known that. How could my not knowing him be best for me?"

With an overly patient nod she didn't feel, Ansley agreed. "Yes, I knew what you wanted. But what we want isn't always what's best for us, sweetheart." She'd learned that the hard way. "And I will not let this man hurt you in any way. I just want to make sure he's good enough for you before I let him anywhere near you."

"But he's my father. And . . . and he's off drugs now. He's clean. He's changed. He's not . . . he's not . . . how could you not tell me about this letter as soon as it came? Oh my God, Mom. How could you not tell me about him as soon as I said his name to you?"

Ansley rubbed at her face, not sure how to answer.

Brooklyn snorted out her impatience. "I don't even know who you are anymore." Bulldozing past Ansley, she stormed toward the exit.

"Brook—"

"Don't talk to me. Don't follow me. I'm staying with Kelsey."

Ansley jumped when the door slammed shut. Covering her mouth with trembling hands, she sank into the chair Brooklyn had just vacated. She didn't go after her, reassured by the fact the girl had at least told her where she would be. Ansley could give her time and space to adjust as long as she knew where her baby was.

Closing her eyes, she wondered if she'd made a mistake by keeping Ward's identity a secret. Or had the mistake come when she hadn't followed Preston's advice and deleted that dreaded email.

When she opened her lashes, that very email blared at her from the screen of her computer. With a growl, she slapped the lid closed and fisted her hands.

"Why won't someone just tell me what the right thing to do is?" Follow respectability and what others would tell her was right, or follow her unreliable heart?

Ward had yet to hear anything back from Ansley. Antsy, he paced the inside of Danny's Haven, looking for something to keep him occupied when he spotted Jace shuffling through games at the Wii station.

"Hey," he said, "Just the guy I was looking for." He pulled a folded piece of paper from his pocket and waved it. "Here's the evidence you demanded. You can now be relieved to know your counselor is clean and free of any drug in his system."

Jace paused and glanced up from his search. He barely eyed the sheet Ward flapped at him. With a negligent shrug, he said, "Cool," and ducked his face back down to read through the DVDs.

"Cool?" Ward fisted the doctor's report in his hand and set it against his hip. "Is that all you've got?" When Jace looked up — his features contorted with confusion — Ward lost it. "You accuse me of falling off the wagon and taking drugs, putting my job and my entire future in jeopardy, not to mention the future of every kid in this place. And now that I've proven you're wrong, all you mumble is cool?"

Jace blinked once before he shrugged and held up a Wii game. "Want to play dance revolution with me?" he offered as if that was some kind of amends.

After staring at him blankly a moment, Ward chuckled out his frustrations. He wasn't sure why he'd expected some kind of apology. Heck, he was just happy Jace and the others hadn't rejected him last night when he'd spilled his deepest, darkest secrets in the circle. Instead of reproof, they'd actually come together and tried to figure out a plan to help him get some face time with Brooklyn. It had shocked and honored him to see how much support he had these days.

"Sure, kid," he said. "Roll out the pad; I'll set up the game."

Jace broke into a grin. "Right on." He thrust the disc at Ward. After jogging across the room, he bent down and pulled the dance pad out from under a couch.

By the time Ward had the game up on the television screen, Jace had dragged out the mat and hooked it up.

Thirty minutes and five songs passed. Hot and sweaty, Ward's nerves had actually begun to loosen. He felt like an absolute fool wiggling around in front of the screen but Jace couldn't stop laughing whenever he put a couple extra bumps to his hips.

"Man, you suck bad." The teen chortled, holding his stomach as he bent forward laughing so hard.

"But my score is higher than yours," Ward taunted and immediately stopped dancing when the song ended. Collapsing onto the nearby couch, he clutched his sore abs and blew out an exhausted breath.

Jace slumped beside him. "I think they're pity points because there's no way you're a better dancer than I am."

"Oh, whatever. Bring it, kid. I'll beat you at another round if you're so convinced I suck."

"You're on, old man."

Without standing up, Jace pointed his controller at the screen and rummaged through the list of songs.

"None of that robot dancing though," Ward warned. Nothing wore him out as fast as trying to keep up with those jerky, strange moves. "I'd hate to totally wipe the floor with your face if we did that again."

"Oh, dream on." Jace rose to the challenge, picking another robotic-sounding song.

Ward closed his eyes and groaned. He'd just let his head fall back on the cushions when a feminine yet hesitant voice said, "Ward?"

He opened his eyes and lifted his face to find his daughter standing ten feet away next to the large flat screen.

"Brooklyn!" He surged to his feet, instantly dizzy from standing so fast. "What . . . what're you doing here?"

"I . . ." Brooklyn glanced at Jace and quickly darted her gaze back to Ward.

Clearing his throat, Jace pointedly turned his attention to the Wii and shut down the game.

With a pair of big blue eyes, Brooklyn looked up at Ward. "Can I talk to you?"

He nodded immediately. "Sure. Of course. Just . . . My office is right over there." He pointed to the opened doorway across the wide commons area. "Go on in. I'll be right there."

She nodded and tentatively turned away. He steadied himself, gulping in copious amounts of oxygen, as she slowly moved off. He couldn't believe his daughter was here, in the same building as him. But even as his brain buzzed with excitement, warning bells clanged through his ears. Brooklyn didn't act like the eager, hopeful, optimistic girl he'd met barely a week ago. Something was wrong. Instantly concerned, he moved to followed her.

"Whoa," Jace said, grabbing Ward's sleeve and jerking him back.

With a frown, Ward glanced at the kid. "What's wrong?"

"What's wrong?" Eyes wide, Jace jabbed his finger after Brooklyn. "That's your daughter?" He whispered the question with an incredulous expression. "Brooklyn Marlow?"

Ward couldn't remember ever mentioning Brooklyn's last name the night before in the group circle. Alarm spread through him.

"Do you guys know each other?"

Jace snorted and shoved Ward in the arm as if he was insane. "Heck, no. Why would she know me?"

"Then how do you know her?" Ward demanded, feeling more and more fatherly by the second.

He liked Jace. He honestly did. But learning an active drug addict knew his daughter's name was not reassuring.

Shrugging, Jace flushed. "Hey, I went to J. Edgar for a few months last year before I was expelled."

That didn't explain how the kid knew his daughter but she didn't know him. Eyes narrowing, Ward stared at Jace and began to tap his toe.

"What?" Jace demanded. "I'm a guy. I make it a point to know the name of every pretty girl in the school I'm attending. And she . . ." He glanced toward the opening of Ward's office only to crane his neck as if he wanted to cop one more peek, "was the prettiest out of, like, all the schools. I so cannot believe she's your kid." He looked Ward up and down and shook his head. "Her mom must be —"

Ward grabbed the front of his shirt. "Stop right there," he growled. "And don't ever check my daughter out again. Got it?"

The teen laughed, letting Ward know his demands were outrageous, but Ward let out a small growl and tugged Jace an inch closer. Jace gulped and nodded, most respectfully. "Got it."

"Good." Ward let go of him and turned away. He entered his office a few seconds later and skidded to a stop when he found Brooklyn standing among his everyday things.

It felt so bizarre. He had a daughter and she was right here in front of him, all grown up and only about half a foot shorter than him. He wanted to tug her into his arms and hug her for, like, an hour.

"Hey," he said, sounding breathless. Feeling breathless. "Sorry, I was . . ." He hooked his thumb over his shoulder, motioning toward Jace, but his explanation for keeping her in here by herself for a couple seconds seemed totally unnecessary.

He blew out a lungful that had been overloading his system. "Have you talked to your mom about . . . about . . . ?"

"About volunteering?" she asked.

Ward wasn't sure if that's what he was asking or not, but since she filled in his sentence with it, he bobbed his head, agreeing.

"Yeah." She folded her hands in her lap

and glanced down at her fingers. "I asked her about it. But that's not why I'm here."

Oh, man. Had Ansley told her who he was? Did she know . . . ?

She looked up, her blue eyes staring straight inside him. "I found the email you wrote her."

"Oh."

Ward shut his office door. He wasn't sure what else to say. But knowing she knew triggered a prickling sensation just under his skin, making every hair on his body stand on end. His scalp tickled with a strange heat. This was his daughter, and she knew he was her father.

"Wow."

She bobbed her head up and down, confirming his sentiment.

For a moment, they merely stared at each other. It felt so surreal, looking at her, seeing himself and Ansley mixed together to form this beautiful, amazing creature, the prettiest girl in all the schools Jace had been kicked out of.

A second later, he realized he should probably say something. "I . . . wait." He shook his head and frowned. "You said you found the letter. She didn't . . . your mom didn't tell you?"

Brooklyn shook her head. He glanced

down at his feet, processing that. Disappointment ran thick through his veins. If Ansley hadn't told her, then . . .

He looked up. "Does she know you know?"

After a slight pause, Brooklyn moved her head up and down with another silent nod.

Ward remembered to exhale again. "And she knows you're here right now? Right?"

"No," his daughter whispered, her eyes wide with apprehension.

His shoulders deflated. That was not a good sign. If Ansley knew Brooklyn had found out about his paternity yet the girl still had to sneak out to come see him, Ansley must not have taken her daughter's newfound knowledge so well.

He sank into a chair and opened his mouth to explain that they should probably call Ansley immediately, when the expression on Brooklyn's face stalled him. She looked so small, and lost. Nervous.

"Are you okay with all this?" he asked. "I mean, it must be quite a shock for you, suddenly knowing who your dad is."

She paused, and he held his breath. Then she nodded. "Yeah. Yeah, I'm okay." Then her lips quivered into an uncertain smile. "I'm kind of excited actually. I know who my dad is now."

He snorted derisively. "Yeah. Disappointing, isn't it?"

Shaking her head, she sent him a brilliant smile. "Not at all. You're alive and drug-free. It's a total relief. It . . ." She choked off suddenly and her lashes went into rapid blink mode. "I'm just so happy you're okay."

When he saw the tears in her eyes, he had to fist his hand and set the trembling appendage against his mouth. He couldn't believe her biggest concern had been for his well-being.

"You shouldn't have been worried about me," he choked out. "Geez, kid. You should be mad I was never around, indignant I made your mom raise you all by herself, hurt I left you."

His daughter merely grinned and wiped at her damp cheeks. "I guess I was just too hopeful you had a good reason for all that. So I'm waiting for your explanation before I decide whether to get mad, hurt, or indignant."

Holy cow, the girl was exactly like her mother. Too good to be true.

On the verge of a break down, he pushed to his feet and turned away. Without answering any of the questions in Brooklyn's eyes, he moved around his desk and picked up the phone. "We should call your mom. If she doesn't want you to have any contact with me, we should respect that."

When her chin quivered, he had to glance away. He set the phone down when he realized he didn't know Ansley's number. Not that he wanted to call her and lose time with his daughter anyway. Fisting his hand, he dug his short nails into his palms, hoping the pain would help ground him. But his eyes still burned.

"She came to see me after I wrote her that email," he explained, staring at the phone in its cradle instead of Brooklyn. When his daughter sprang to her feet, he glanced up. Her eyes widened and filled with what he could only guess was hope, so he nodded. "She wanted some time to decide whether it was a good idea if we should get to know each other or not. So, until then, it's probably best if we don't . . ."

He couldn't finish the sentence. He couldn't send his child away. But would Ansley sic the law on him if she found out about their visit?

Letting out a tortured sound, Brooklyn bunched up her chin and whispered, "Don't you want to get to know me?"

God. Now his own chin was quivering. He closed his eyes. "Please." The word grated from his throat. "Don't think that.

This isn't about what I want at all. I would be honored to know every little detail about you. I crave to be a part of your life. But you don't know everything that happened. You don't understand."

"Then make me understand," she insisted, her voice desperate as she moved closer to him and actually reached out both her hands to touch him.

In response, he moved toward her too, wanting nothing but to enfold her into his arms and envelop his precious child in nothing but a safety net of love. But his sanity returned. He jerked away from her at that last second. She stumbled to a stop and gaped up at him as if he'd just slapped her.

A sob hiccupped from her throat, and tears slid seamlessly down her cheeks, one right after another.

It tore him in half.

"Brooklyn." Her name burned its way up his windpipe.

"Just tell me," she begged, her shoulders heaving as she wept openly.

He licked his dry lips, helpless to deny her anything. Even the truth. "I spent three years in jail for raping your mother," he whispered.

Chapter Nine

Ansley readied herself for bed, morosely applying lotion to her arms and face as she listened to the silence of the house around her. She'd never known how much more noise living with even just one other person could fill a home. She distinctly noticed how absent her daughter was.

About half an hour after Brooklyn had stormed off, Ansley had called Kelsey's mom to make sure Brooklyn had showed up. When the other mom had assured her, Brooklyn had arrived safely and gone straight to Kelsey's room, Ansley had relaxed marginally. But she still worried.

She could handle her daughter being mad at her when she didn't always get her way. But knowing Brooklyn might be hurt because she'd made a mistake bothered her to no end. Hunting up her cell phone, she began to type in a quick text, just to wish Brooklyn a good night and let her know she loved her, plus tell her they could talk any time she wanted. But she heard the back door open before she was finished composing her message.

Instant relief flooded her. Her baby had come home.

She waited a minute, listening to Brooklyn move through the house and enter her own room, closing her door. Then, she hurried to out of her bedroom, ready to make amends, ready to be open and honest about everything.

Gently rapping her knuckles against the door, she called, "Brooklyn?" When no one answered, Ansley frowned. "Honey?" She grasped the doorknob and turned.

Her daughter sat on the bed, her hands in her lap, her knees pressed together and her head bowed with her curled shoulders shaking violently. When Brooklyn lifted her face, Ansley saw the tears trailing down her cheeks, and she sucked in a quick breath.

"Oh my God. What's wrong?" She hurried into the room and sat next to Brooklyn, taking her hands. Brooklyn sniffed and wiped at her cheeks. From the red ringing her eyes, Ansley could tell she'd been crying awhile.

"Brooklyn?" She smoothed the girl's dark locks out of her face before she mopped at the tears as well. "What happened, sweetheart? Did you have a fight with Kelsey too?"

When she pulled her teen in for a hug, Brooklyn went willingly, wrapping her arms around Ansley's neck and squeezing tight.

"Is it true?" Brooklyn whispered the tear-clogged question, soaking Ansley's neck.

Utterly baffled, Ansley shook her head. "Is what true?"

"Did he . . . did he really, you know . . . rape you?"

Ansley jerked back. When her daughter stared at her with a probing gaze, she blinked.

"Ward?" she asked. As Brooklyn nodded, she closed her eyes and pressed her fingers to her forehead. "No, of course not. Why would you even think that?"

Her brow furrowing in confusion, Brooklyn rasped, "Because that's what he told me. He said . . . he said . . ." She hiccupped and wiped her face.

Mouth falling open, Ansley gaped. "He told you he . . . ? Wait a second. When did he tell you anything?"

Cringing, Brooklyn mumbled, "Tonight."

"You went to see him? But Kelsey's mom said you were there."

"I was. I left. I went to Danny's Haven. I

had to see him. But he said . . ."

Ansley squeezed the bridge of her nose between her fingers. "I told you not to go there, Brooklyn. It's not safe, and —"

"Why would he say it if it wasn't true?" Brooklyn cried.

Ansley clenched her teeth. "It's a big, complicated mess. I don't even know how to explain it. My parents were so certain he took advantage of me, but no one knows for sure. Not even Ward and I."

Brooklyn sniffed and shook her head. "That doesn't make any sense. How could you not know?"

When Ansley hesitated, her daughter squeezed her hands hard. "Please, Mom. I need to know how I was created. Just tell me."

Letting out a shaky breath, Ansley nodded. "Yes, all right. He's already told you enough to warrant some explanation." She closed her eyes and began. "Ward and I met when I was fifteen. He was eighteen. And he showed up out of the blue one Wednesday at my midweek Bible study class."

Brooklyn made a relieved sound in the back of her throat. "So, he . . . you two actually knew each other before?"

Ansley sent her a strange look. "Of course. Did you think we were complete strangers, and he accosted me in a dark alley one stormy night?"

Her cheeks flushed as Brooklyn ducked her face. "Well, I don't know. He made it sound like —"

Clenching her teeth, Ansley growled out a low sound, promising herself Ward Gemmell would pay for hurting her daughter like this. "I have no idea what he told you, but here's my version of the story. It's not pretty, but I'll be nothing but completely honest with you because you obviously need to know the truth."

Brooklyn shuddered as she nodded, already looking calmer and reassured. "Thank you."

"At the time, I thought he was a Christian and had been one his entire life. Like me. It wasn't until later, recently actually, that I learned that had been the first time he'd ever stepped foot inside a church, that he wasn't the kind of person I thought he was at all."

She shook her head, baffled she'd ever fallen for his good boy act. She'd been such a stupid, naïve girl.

"So what happened?" Brooklyn pressed.

"After the first Bible meeting, I followed him outside and started up a conversation." Her face heated as she blushed. "He was cute and seemed bashful. We ended up walking to this fast food restaurant down the street, where he bought us a couple of cold drinks. We sat in a booth across from each other. I think we talked for at least an hour that first night. After that, we sat by each other at every study group. We shared a Bible to read from, and things just . . . progressed. Every week, I'd show up a little earlier so I could see him, and every week, he'd be waiting outside the church for me to arrive. Then after one meeting when we went to get our weekly soda after the group meeting, I just couldn't help myself any longer. I kissed him."

Brooklyn's jaw dropped. "Whoa, Mom. You kissed him? That's so bold for you."

If Ansley's cheeks were hot before, they were scalding now. She nodded and then grinned. She'd been a lot bolder when she'd been fifteen and clueless. Still. "I know. It was a crazy thing for me to do then too. But I was so over the moon for him. I thought I was in love. He was just so . . . so devoted."

Brooklyn wrinkled her nose. "Devoted?"

Ansley laughed. "Yeah. Whenever I was around him, he paid attention to no one but me. It was as if nothing was as important to him as what I had to say. Like he adored me. And the way he always watched me . . .

Oh Brooklyn, he looked so fascinated, as if I was actually an interesting person. It made me feel so special."

No one had ever made her feel that way before or since.

"So . . . he liked you as much as you liked him then?"

Nodding, Ansley let out a breath where tight pressure had built in her chest. But every time she remembered those first magical weeks with Ward, an echo of the anticipation to see him again swirled through her. Those days had been every young, innocent girl's fantasy romance come true.

"What happened?" Brooklyn repeated the dreaded question.

"Well . . . after the first kiss, we were inseparable. We talked on the phone almost every night. We held hands just about every second we were together. But we never made it past a closed-mouthed kiss. It was all so very sweet. So innocent. I think . . ."

She swallowed before continuing. "I think he realized how inexperienced I was because he never pushed, never pressured for more like you'd think every teenage boy would do. He just seemed content to be with me. I was the one who instigated every new intimate facet of the relationship. I kissed him first. I took his hand to hold. I said I wanted to meet his friends."

Brooklyn's charmed grin faltered, obviously catching something telling in Ansley's gaze, or maybe in her voice. "That's where it went bad, huh? With his friends?"

Ansley nodded. "Apparently Ward was a completely different person when I wasn't around. He and his friends did drugs and got into just about every kind of illegal mischief known to mankind. When I first asked if I could meet his friends, I remember him blanching. I mean, his face literally drained of color. He made lame excuses for a while, but I kept pressing. And then one day, one of his friends actually showed up at the restaurant where we got our drinks after our Bible Study lessons.

"Ward immediately became stiff and tense, not at all how I thought he'd act around one of his closest companions. But his buddy kept teasing him about me. I wasn't sure what was going on, but I assumed he and his friend had recently argued or something. Though now, I wonder if Ward had been uncomfortable because he was afraid I would figure out what he was really like."

"What was he really like?"

Ansley licked her dry lips. "After everything happened, my parents found out his criminal record. By the time he'd met me, he'd gotten busted twice for petty theft, three times for possession of drugs, once for vandalism, once for brawling, and three times for public intoxication."

"Wow," Brooklyn whispered. "He really did put on a good boy front for you."

Ansley sniffed in chagrin. "Yeah. I was blind to all of it too. But honestly, he didn't once do anything to ever make me think he was like that. He was always so clean-cut around me. Never cussed, never said anything derogatory or cruel about anyone else. He always bought our drinks, and opened doors for me, and he . . . he was just a complete gentleman."

"Did the friend clue you in to his true identity?" Brooklyn asked.

"No. Not that day. But he did invite us to attend a get-together, as he called it. Ward immediately declined for both of us. When I asked him why we couldn't go, he stuttered around, not really answering me. Finally, after I kept pestering him, he said it wasn't the kind of party I'd like. But I told him I wanted to get to know his friends . . . get to know him better. He continued to tell me he didn't want to go. But I was like, oh we're going. And he never could tell me no, so . . ." She shrugged. "We went."

When she glanced at Brooklyn, Brooklyn's gaze said she knew the bad part of the story was about to come. "What happened?"

"Even as we approached the door to the run-down house where the party took place, Ward tried to talk me out of going. I could hear the loud, thumping music and raised voices. For the first time, I felt hesitant, but we were already there, so I strode inside, grasping Ward's hand and pulling him along with me."

Like a brave, stupid idiot.

"Once we entered, though, I jerked to an immediate halt. I think everyone was drinking alcohol, and all of them were clearly underage. People all around me were cussing. And this sickly sweet smell filled the air.

"My eyes turned the size of quarters when I saw a couple making out on a couch against the wall . . . without much clothing on. Ward clutched my hand so hard I'm surprised he didn't leave a bruise. He pulled me close and I clung to him, very, very hesitant by that point. When he leaned toward me and yelled in my ear, asking if I was ready to go, I immediately nodded yes. He looked into my eyes then, and I saw guilt. That's when I knew; he wasn't quite everything I thought he was.

"We started for the door, but his friend intercepted us and thrust a cup at me. I didn't drink it at first, wondering if there was alcohol in it. Ward took it and sipped before sending me a reassured smile and yelling into my ear that it was just soda. After that, I gulped. My throat was so dry; I was so nervous. Ward tried to get away from his talkative friend and get me out of there, but more and more friends appeared, introducing themselves. They all had such potty mouths. I remembering wondering how Ward could stand to talk to them."

"Something was in the drink, wasn't it?" Brooklyn broke in.

Ansley nodded. "Yes. Rohypnol."

Mouth dropping open, her daughter gasped. "Oh my God. You were drugged? Was it . . . ? Did Ward drug you?"

Ansley shook her head. "He insisted it wasn't him."

"But you don't believe him?"

"Oh, I do. Even after I learned what kind of person he really was, I couldn't forget how he'd always treated me. No one with that much care and respect inside him could be that awful. Even at the party, when I told him I felt sick, he was frantic to find me a bathroom, or even the exit to get us out of there. I remember how the room pitched, and I grew dizzier. It felt like we were in some creepy, scary maze and couldn't find our way out. I heard him curse for the first time then. He grabbed one of his friends and yanked him close, demanding to know how to get us out of there. I think the friend was high. He let out this strange, high-pitched laugh and told us to follow him. When the friend pointed toward a darkened doorway, Ward latched his hand tight around mine, and led the way inside. But when he turned on the light, his friends slammed the door behind us and yelled, 'enjoy.' They'd led us to a bedroom . . . and locked us inside together."

Brooklyn's mouth dropped open.

Rubbing her hands up and down the sides of her arms, Ansley continued. "I remember Ward yelling and pounding on the door. He rammed his shoulder against it a few times. All these foul curses flooded out of him as he threatened his friends and demanded they let us out. He sounded like a complete stranger. I got scared and backed up until I bumped into the bed. Then I sat on the mattress and began to cry. After he pushed a dresser in front of the door, Ward came and sat next to me, telling me everything would be okay. He wouldn't let anyone get to me. He put his arms around me, and I cried into his shoulder. The last thing I remember was clutching him and bawling into his shirt as we lay down on the bed next to each other."

"Wow," Brooklyn whispered, appearing shell shocked. "You don't remember anything after that?"

Ansley shook her head. "I don't know how long I was out, but Ward was the one who shook me awake. Someone was pounding on the door, yelling something about the police. Or maybe it was the police pounding, telling us to let them in. I don't know. But the cops were definitely there. I couldn't focus past Ward. He was crying and trembling. I asked him what was wrong, but he merely thrust this bundle into my arms and turned away. When I looked down at what I held, I realized it was my clothes."

"Oh, no." Brooklyn covered her mouth with both hands.

Ansley nodded. "I asked him what happened but he said he didn't know. He thought someone must've spiked my drink, and since he drank some of it too, it affected him as well. He lost his memory, just as I did. He couldn't seem to stop crying, which scared me more than anything. So I started crying. I tried to put my clothes on, but I kept fumbling. Ward finally noticed and helped me. He kept apologizing, only to pause and assured me he'd never do anything to hurt me, before he started apologizing again. Once we got my clothes back in order, he shoved aside the dresser and let the police in.

"He tried to explain to them what had happened, but he was so upset, he would stop every few words and beg them to help me, to call my parents. They took us to the hospital, where we were both drug tested and, yes, we both tested positive for the date rape drug, rohypnol. I also discovered I was no longer a virgin there. My parents took me home after that. I don't know what happened to Ward. I didn't see him or hear from him again for over a month . . . after I realized I was pregnant."

Brooklyn leaned forward, totally engrossed in her mother's story. "What'd you do?"

"I went looking for him. It's possible he might've tried to see me but my parents kept him away. I'm not sure. They never wanted to hear from him again. I did though. Even after what happened, I waited every day for him to come to me. But when I found out about you, I stopped waiting and started searching.

"I sneaked out of the house and found his mom and her husband's address, only to be told he no longer lived there. When I asked his mother where I could find him, she didn't know, didn't seem to care. She was . . . very bitter and acted glad to see him gone. After that, I asked around. When I remembered the name of one of his friends, I asked about the friend until I found where he lived. Fortunately, Ward had been staying with him, so I didn't have to look any farther.

"When I got to the friend's house, it was just after school. Ward was high. He reeked of that same awful smell I remembered from the party and was smoking . . . I don't know, a joint, I guess. He was lying, stretched out on top of this dingy old picnic table in the friend's backyard with his feet crossed at the ankles as he stared up at the limbs of the tree above him. I walked all the way up to him before he even noticed me. When he saw me, he smiled at me with a strange, dazed kind of grin. Then his eyes welled with tears and he said, 'you were never supposed to find out about me.'

"I asked, 'find out what?' and he answered, 'what I really am.' It all came out then, he told me every awful thing he'd ever done. But strangely, I wasn't as horrified as I knew I should be. I remembered how wonderful he'd always been to me and was so sure there was still some of that good person inside him. So I begged him to just change, to become the person I knew him to be. I told him I needed the Ward I knew because I was going to have a baby."

She grinned at Brooklyn. "It was so very dramatic."

Brooklyn didn't return the smile. "What'd he say?"

"When he heard I was pregnant? He started to laugh. Tears streamed down his face, but he kept laughing. Finally, he said something along the lines of, 'That figures.' Then he told me the best thing I could do for my baby was stay far, far away from a mess like him. I was so disappointed, so crushed. I ran home and cried for a week. Another week later, he showed up on my parents' doorstep. He looked sober and drug-free. He even wore one of those clean-cut outfits I'd always see him in at the study group.

"When he told me he wanted to clean up and help me with you, I finally got excited about you for the first time. We were going to be a family, a real family. I ran inside after he left and told my parents. They weren't so excited, though. They kept talk-ing about restraining orders and pressing charges. I just wanted Ward to come back and make everything better again. But another week passed before I saw him while I was walking home from school.

"This time, he wasn't sober. I don't know if he was drunk, or high, or both, but he was not the Ward I knew. He was rougher, more aggressive. He didn't hurt me, of course, but his abrasive behavior scared me, and I started crying.

"Instead of apologizing, he got mad and demanded to know why I was so scared. He said I should know better, I should know he'd never hurt me. But he was the Ward I didn't understand, so I pulled away from him and ran home. And . . . that's the last time I ever saw or heard from him until you came home the other day and said his name to me."

Ansley stopped talking, feeling drained, body, mind and soul. Her entire history with Ward now lay like an eerie echo, smacking against the walls of Brooklyn's quiet room. As her daughter sat quietly beside her, holding Ansley's hand, she studied the posters and shelves crammed with stuffed animals. The bedroom was comfortable and familiar, and yet it felt different now. Everything felt different, because Brooklyn finally knew her origins.

"Do you hate me?" She wasn't sure why the question croaked its way from her lips.

A lifetime of insecurities simply rushed to the surface and she blurted out the words before she could stop herself.

Brooklyn's fingers tightened around hers as she whirled to gape at Ansley. "Why would I hate you?"

"I don't know. I was so stupid and naïve. I should've listened to him when he said he didn't want to go to that party."

"And he should've kept refusing to take you," her daughter countered with an outraged scowl. "You weren't naïve, Mom. You were fifteen!"

"But you're not much older than that," Ansley felt compelled to argue. "And I can't even imagine you being so dim-witted." She stared into her child's intelligent blue eyes. There was a certain wisdom, an age-old maturity in Brooklyn that Ansley sometimes felt she still lacked. Something she must've inherited from Ward. "You would've learned about his background far faster than I would've. You never would've fallen for his innocent act. You —"

Brooklyn blushed and lifted her hand. "Mom. You don't know that for certain. Besides," she shrugged, looking a little rueful, "it sounds like he was pretty convincing. And maybe not all of what he did and said was an act."

Ansley sucked in a breath when she took in the expression on her daughter's face, the gleam of hope glittering like bright crystals from her cerulean eyes.

Fear lodged in her throat as she realized Brooklyn was wishing the very same thing Ansley had been wishing for the past seventeen years — that Ward Gemmell had honestly never meant to hurt her, that he'd never known anything had been in her drink, that he'd truly changed for the better, and that there was a good reason he'd stayed away all these years.

"Listen to me," Ansley said, squeezing Brooklyn's fingers tight. "I know you want to trust him, and I know you want to get to know him. But he's been deceptive in the past. He's lied and he's broken the law. I don't want you to go around him again until I've checked his situation out and have decided you can be completely safe around him. Okay?"

For a moment, Brooklyn looked like she wanted to rebel. Her eyes grew wide and bright. Her chin trembled, and her lips pressed flat. But in the end, she gave a grudging nod.

"Okay, Mom. I trust you."

That was a start. But Ansley wasn't sure if she could trust herself.

CHAPTER TEN

"You shouldn't have told her."

Ward jolted in his chair as that voice — Ansley's voice — whipped through him. He jerked his face up to see her framed in the opened doorway of his office. With her purse securely hooked over her shoulder, she was able to fist her hands down at her sides quite nicely. She stepped into the room and closed the door. Another jarring bolt of anticipation rattled him from head to toe.

The two of them, alone, should not give him a thrill, but his nerve endings danced with excitement, beyond pleased she didn't seem the slightest bit wary about closeting herself inside a small, cramped office with him.

He licked his lips as she sat down, so he stayed seated himself, worried that coming out from behind the desk might make her more uncomfortable.

God, she looked so elegant sitting there. Her back straight, her chin held defiantly high, her shoulders jutting out with a firm yet feminine determination. Ready to battle him.

He glanced away. "She was going to keep coming back. I could see it in her eyes. And I thought if she knew, then it might . . . I don't know, scare her off until you made a decision."

She narrowed beautiful brown eyes. "And it didn't occur to you that hearing she was a product of rape might upset her, might scar her into thinking her entire existence was based upon a brutal event, might make her feel like she was worth less of a person now?"

His face drained of color. "Oh," he whispered. "No. Oh my God, I didn't even think of that. I . . . is she okay?"

Ansley pressed her lips together tight. "She was very upset and it took a lot of talking for me to calm her down. But . . . I still don't understand why. My God, Ward. To her, you made it sound as if you were some dark, hooded stranger who'd attacked me in an alleyway on my way home from church."

His mouth twitched, but he managed to keep the smile in. To him, that wasn't too far from the truth. "What did you expect me to do; put some rose-colored slant on it to make it look better than it really was?"

"Well, it certainly wasn't as bad as you made it seem."

"Oh, come on, Ansley." He barked out a harsh laugh. "Is there a good side of rape?"

"Why are you calling it that? Your blood tested positive with signs of rohypnol too, so I consider you just as much a victim of that night as I was."

He squinted at her and shook his head. If she really believed that, then why had she sent him to jail for rape? "No. I don't care how blitzed I might've been. I took advantage of you —"

"And how do you really know that? You remember as much of it as I do. Which is absolutely nothing. For all we know, I'm the one who seduced you —"

"Please." He groaned and rolled his eyes, wondering why in God's name she was arguing about this with him. "I was eighteen. You weren't. That's statutory, right there, whether it was consensual or not. Besides, I took you to that party when I knew perfectly well what kind of things happened there."

"Yeah, after I pressured you into it. You tried to talk me out of it as I recall."

He threw his hand into the air, surrendering, and fell back in his chair. "You know, this whole discussion is moot. We can't —"

"Yes, it is," she interrupted before he could continue. "Because despite what happened seventeen years ago, it's what you did last night that concerns me." She drew up her shoulders sharp and taut, and looked him straight in the eye. "I wanted to believe you had changed. I wanted to believe you were no longer the type of person to say whatever you had to say — truth or lie — to get another to do what you wanted them to do. But after the way you hurt Brooklyn last night, I don't think this is a good idea."

He frowned. Wait . . . what? "You don't think what is a good idea?"

"This . . ." She gestured vaguely around the room. "You getting involved in her life. I think we should just keep things how they are. No contact between you two. At all."

Ward gaped at her, thunderstruck.

The deep instinctive need for him to fight for his daughter made him blurt out "But —" Except he didn't get any farther than that.

Ansley pinned him with her steely brown gaze, and the pain in her eyes rendered him mute.

"You didn't see how upset she was." Her

hoarse voice scraped through him, grating against his soul, stripping him raw. "She was so . . ." She shook her head and closed her lashes. "I've never seen her so devastated. I'm not sure if she'll ever get over it."

"I'm sorry," he whispered. It sounded inadequate to his ears as his voice echoed around the dim room. When she opened her lashes, he could tell it must've sounded just as inadequate to her too.

She licked her lips and spoke in a low, gruff tone. "I would prefer it if you stayed away from her. For good."

Dry eyes burning, Ward stared. Her words clanged through him, but he found it impossible to believe them. For the past seventeen years, he'd been fighting and struggling, and giving it his all to become a better person, to become a person good enough to be Brooklyn's father. All those years, all that work, and in the end, none of it mattered.

He wanted to blame Hollywood. The movies showed how hard work and effort always won in the end. As long as you put everything you had into it, you could get whatever your heart desired.

Yet, there he sat, staring at Ansley Marlow, and he was being rejected from her life, rejected from her daughter's life. Rejected from the life he craved to live.

Everything inside him begged, please, please don't do this to me. I can work harder, do better. He tried to contain the entreaty, but some of it — or maybe all of it — reflected in his face because she squeezed her eyes closed and turned her head aside.

He blinked, fighting back the moisture pooling in his tear ducts, and cleared his throat.

"Okay," he managed to grate out, but it didn't sound very coherent so he had to try again. "Okay." He straightened his spine as if that would help boost his plummeting morale. "I get it." But he couldn't look at her as the words vacated his mouth.

"I'm sorry," she said, her low voice quivering.

Dear God, she better not cry. If she started crying, he'd sob like a little baby.

"No." He shook his head. "Don't apologize. It's okay. I understand. It . . . it's the right decision, Ansley. I know I'm not any kind of ideal dad."

He caught a glimpse of her in his peripheral vision. Her face lowered as she clasped her hands tight in her lap. "She's going to have one anyway. A dad, I mean. I . . . I've decided to get married so Brooklyn's going to have a father figure soon, and . . ."

His eyes flared wide. She was getting married?

That news was almost as devastating as learning he was being denied access to his child. Two blows. One setting. How was he going to survive this?

Yet there he sat. There he kept breathing. He didn't topple over into dust, and his world didn't stop in its tracks.

He only wished it would.

He nodded. "I . . . well, that's good. I mean, congratulations." The lies slid so easily off his tongue, he was surprised the foul organ didn't fall out of his mouth for such deceit.

But from the corner of his eye, he saw Ansley nod in agreement. "He's a . . . a surgeon," she said. "So Brooklyn will never want for anything."

While Ward was a minimum wage drug counselor for troubled teens. Yeah, he got it.

"Well, then." He blew out a breath, wishing she'd leave before he fell apart. "It sounds like she'll be in good hands. I can be glad for that." His knee started jiggling, and no thought in his head was strong enough to command it to stop.

Ansley nodded again. "He's a very good man."

And Ward had a bad past and arrest

record longer than most people's shopping lists.

His control slipped as he gnashed his teeth. If she didn't leave soon —

"I should go," she rushed out the words, popping to her feet.

He stood as well. "I . . ." He lifted his face to watch her back as she fled his office. When the door shut quietly behind her, he closed his eyes. "Goodbye, Ansley. Have a good life."

CHAPTER ELEVEN

"You're late!"

Ansley nearly jolted out of her skin as she was accosted as soon as she opened the door. Curse it. She'd been hoping Brooklyn might be at Kelsey's house when she got home.

But her daughter raced to her as soon as she opened the back door. "Where were you? Did you go see . . . him?"

Her nerves were still shredded after seeing the crushed expression on Ward's face, so Ansley waited until she'd hung her purse and keys from the wall hook and removed her coat before blowing out a cleansing breath. "Yes. Yes, I saw him."

"You did?" Glowing, Brooklyn squealed and jumped up and down as she clasped Ansley's hands. Her giddy grin was so enthusiastic, Ansley had to turn her face aside and briefly close her eyes. "So, when can I see him? Did you guys, like, set up visitation rights or whatever?"

"I . . ." Gulping, Ansley tried to find the right words to say as gently as possible. "I . . ."

"Oh, my God." Brooklyn gasped and covered her mouth. Her eyes filled with shocked horror. "You decided against me ever seeing him again."

Blinking rapidly, Ansley nodded. "Yes. Yes, I did."

"But . . ." The same frozen, bowled-over expression that had lined Ward's face when she'd told him now mirrored across Brooklyn's.

Not for the first time, indecision warred inside her. She'd done this to keep her child from being hurt. But the two huge crocodile tears snaking down Brooklyn's crushed features didn't seem to make her daughter look unhurt in the least.

"Don't . . . don't you want me to have a father?" the teen sobbed.

Ansley straightened her shoulders and tightened her resolve. "Yes. Actually, yes I do. Which brings me to another topic I need to discuss with you. Preston proposed to me."

"Proposed?" Brooklyn blinked blankly, another round of huge tears slipping from her blue eyes. "Proposed what?"

166

Ansley gave a startled laugh. "Marriage. He proposed marriage."

This time, the repulsion in Brooklyn's expression caught Ansley by surprise. "But he's so old."

"Old?" Ansley's mouth fell open. "But you've never said anything about his age before."

"Because he never proposed before," Brooklyn wailed. "Oh my God. I didn't think you guys were seriously dating. I thought it was just lonely companionship. An only-friends kind of thing. I've never even seen you two kiss."

Exasperated, Ansley rolled her eyes. "We kiss all the time."

Brooklyn rolled her eyes right back. "Quick pecks on the mouth do not count. Grandma and I give each other quick pecks on the mouth. Those are not kiss-kisses. Seriously, Mom, have you even frenched Dr. Jackson?"

Face instantly scalding hot, Ansley pulled her shoulders back in outrage. "That is none of your business."

The teen lifted her brows with a knowing arch. "I didn't think so."

Not needing a new confrontation after the encounter she'd just survived with Ward, Ansley brushed past Brooklyn and rounded the bar to enter the kitchen and begin supper. She'd left a bowl of chicken to thaw in the refrigerator before leaving for work that morning. When she pulled it out, she found it still frozen solid.

Wanting to fall to pieces because nothing was going how she wanted it to tonight, she marched to the sink and began to run water over the meat. She's thaw it one way or another.

Brooklyn hopped onto the counter next to her, watching her silently. Able to deal with her daughter's screaming or yelling better than her silent scrutiny, Ansley squirmed before shutting off the water and lifting her face.

"So you don't want me to marry him, is that what you're saying? You don't want Preston for a father."

The teen merely stared at her. "I already have a father."

Ansley threw her hands into the air, frustrated. "Yeah. One you don't even know! One that left us seventeen years ago and only came back into our lives because you approached him first."

With the careless shrug of a typically young adult, Brooklyn didn't answer.

Gritting her teeth, Ansley scowled. "You're not going to give up on this until I let you have your way and see him again, are you?"

The girl smiled, even though her lashes were still damp from her tears. At least she no longer looked crushed. In fact, she looked a little too happy, as if she knew something Ansley didn't. "I know you, Mom," she said, her smirk full of cocky victory. "You'll give in because you want to. And you won't marry Dr. Jackson because you don't want to."

Though a bolt of panic pierced her, Ansley lifted an eyebrow. "Oh, you think you know me so well, huh?"

Her daughter nodded. "I know you better than anyone. You may want to do what you think is good and proper, but your heart always wins out."

The words rattled her. Ansley buried her face in her hands and leaned her elbows on the counter beside Brooklyn. When the girl began to rub her back in slow, soothing circles, she shuddered, wondering when her sixteen-year-old had become so wise?

"And what if my heart is wrong?" she whispered.

Brooklyn rubbed her back a second longer before patting it with reassurance. "I watched a video on his website."

Ansley sucked in a harsh breath. "I saw it too."

"He talked about you."

Biting her lip, Ansley nodded.

"Then how could you think he wasn't safe for me to be around after watching that? How could you think he wasn't changed, wasn't a better person?"

Straightening, Ansley dropped her hands to her sides. "Because he was just that captivating seventeen years ago. Brooklyn, please trust me. I know he fascinates you just as much as he did me; I can see it on your face. I know you want him to be the person he appears to be on that video, but —"

Brooklyn jumped off the counter and set her fisted hand against her hips. "Why can't you just believe he is that person?"

"Because I've already lived through this once. And I know for a certainty that I can't trust my emotions or feelings at all whenever it comes to Ward Gemmell."

Brooklyn gasped, her mouth falling open. "Oh my God. You still like him."

Ansley shook her head even as she sniffed and admitted, "Whatever stupid crush I still have isn't trustworthy. We have to think with our heads here. And rationally, Grandma and Grandpa would have a cow if they found out we'd let him anywhere near us. Preston's already told me it would be a stupid mistake. Heck, any stranger off the street would say —"

"What do you care what other people think, Mom? This is about us, not them."

"I care because our safety and protection and happiness is their main concern. And if they would be concerned about this, then —"

"Oh, please. Grandma and Grandpa are a little too overprotective if you ask me. And Dr. Jackson is just a stick in the mud. You want to get to know him again just as much as I do. I can see it on your face. So why can't we just give him a chance?"

Ansley blinked away a sudden sting of tears. "I just don't want you to get hurt." She knew she should confess that she didn't want to get hurt again either. But she could deal with her own pain. It was her daughter's pain — if Ward should happen to hurt Brooklyn — that she couldn't handle.

Brooklyn's determined expression softened. With a smile, she leaned forward and kissed Ansley on the cheek. "I love you too, Mom. But you can't keep me from never getting hurt. And this is one risk I'm willing to take. I want to. Please."

Swallowing past the lump in her throat, Ansley nodded. "Okay. All right. I'll think about it again then," she promised.

CHAPTER TWELVE

Ward still wanted to shrivel into a little pile of dust and blow off into nothing by nine that evening when his doorbell rang.

"That's probably the pizza," Care called from the kitchen.

Ward shook his head. "You ordered pizza?"

"We're starving," Desi whined from next to him on the couch. Ripping away the bowl of popcorn she'd set on his lap five minutes ago, she nudged him to get up. "Well . . ." She urged. "It's your house. You pay."

He blinked and sent her an incredulous look. He hadn't ordered the pizza. He didn't want pizza. He didn't even want all the company. But Desi, then Care, then a couple other co-workers had shown up and wouldn't leave.

"Oh, all right," Desi grumbled, lifting up one hip to retrieve a wallet from her back pocket. A second later, she thrust a twenty into his unsuspecting hand. "But I'm only paying because you're all heartbroken and stuff."

He shook his head. Her aptitude in the sympathy department needed some work. But actually, her no-nonsense manner probably helped him more than a there-there, pat-on-the-back act would.

With a handful of cash, he opened the door, expecting to see a delivery boy.

Ansley lifted her face, her eyes huge and scared. "I think I messed up," she blurted out the confession on a breathless wheeze.

His mouth fell open. He couldn't believe she was here, standing in his doorway.

"Is it the pizza?" Care demanded, coming up behind him.

He jumped, then turned slightly to look at her.

Ansley saw the other woman and immediately scurried a step back. "I'm sorry. I didn't realize you had company. I . . . I'm sorry." She turned to flee, but this time he refused let her escape.

Shooting out his door, he grasped her arm. "Ansley, no! Wait."

She stumbled a step, then hesitated before turning back to him. "I'm sorry, I . . ." But her face fell and tears flooded her cheeks. "I don't know what I'm doing."

Watching her fall apart steadied him. He wasn't sure why, it should've sent him right over the edge along with her. But her tears brought out a protective instinct in him, and his own problems suddenly didn't matter.

He pulled her into his embrace and held her close, needing to comfort her.

Over her trembling shoulder, Desi waved at him to get his attention. Crowded in his doorway next to Care, she gawked from owl eyes. "We're just going to . . . yeah . . . scram now."

Ansley didn't seem to notice the exodus from his apartment as he shifted her to the side so the half a dozen people who'd invited themselves over could escape out the opened door. When she lifted her face a minute later to wipe at her wet cheeks, she seemed surprised they were alone.

"You were having a party?"

"No." He shook his head, then flushed. "Well, it certainly wasn't planned, and it was more like a pity party. A couple friends started appearing on my doorstep, thinking they could cheer me up, and before I knew it, my apartment was crowded." He gave a rueful shrug.

She wiped at her other cheek and studied him. "You have good friends."

His face relaxed as he nodded. "Yeah, I do. These days anyway."

"And they were here to cheer you up?" she repeated, finally catching onto that phrase.

He winced, then shooed her into the apartment so he could shut the door.

Her big brown eyes bored into him as he closed them in his living room together. "Did I upset you that much?"

"What? No." He shook his head to deny it but he couldn't look at her. Then again, he couldn't not look at her. When he turned back, his resolve crumbled. He bunched his chin and squinted his eyes to keep from starting another monsoon.

"Ward?" she whispered, seeing right through him.

He began to blink rapidly. "I just . . ." His voice broke. Glancing down at his hands, he watched them tremble. "I worked seventeen years for this moment, and I didn't even realize it until it was here. But I have been struggling to overcome my past, my inner devil, my arrest record, to become the man good enough to be the father to a child I wasn't even completely certain existed. I've even been putting a portion of my paycheck into a savings account for her. For years. To learn that's not good enough . . .

it just . . . it took the wind out of my sails, you know. I . . ."

"Ward, I'm sorry."

"No, no. Don't be sorry. You made the best decision for your daughter. I don't blame you for that. I will never blame you. For anything. I know what I was. I know what I am now. I mean, I could never compete with a doctor. You made the right decision. All I ever did was hurt you."

She shook her head. "No. The only thing you did to really hurt me was disappear from my life for seventeen years."

His eyes filled. Gah, he hated being unable to control the stupid tears today. Wiping at them furiously, he breathed out a strangled breath. "And here, for the last seventeen years, I thought disappearing from your life was the best thing I ever could've done for you. I thought it was what you wanted. Please don't tell me I was wrong."

She looked him dead in the eye. "You were wrong."

He frowned. "But —"

She sighed out a long, dramatic exhalation. "Are you ever going to tell me why?"

He shook his head confused. "Why what?"

Her eyes bloomed with disbelief. "Why what?" she thundered as her fingers curled

176

into fists. "Why you left and never came back. Why, Ward, why did you abandon us?"

His mouth dropped open. "I . . ." was all he could think to say, feeling blank. Had she really, honestly wanted him to return after he got out of jail? It didn't seem possible. She'd never even visited him while he was behind bars.

Nostrils flaring and chest heaving with obvious ire, she glared him down. "I waited, and waited and waited for you. I even looked for you. But it was like you disappeared off the face of the earth."

It felt like a Mack truck had slammed into his chest and left him pinned, stealing all his oxygen. He could only stare at her, perplexed. "I don't understand."

"What's to understand?" she cried, more upset than he'd ever seen her. "You left when I needed you most and never came back. And now that I finally have a handle on my life and know I can raise my daughter alone, you waltz right back in as if the last seventeen years never happened. How dare you?"

"Ansley —" he started, knowing he needed to calm her down before they continued this conversation. But she obviously wanted nothing to do with calm. Angry, frustrated tears filled her eyes. "I asked for you when she was born. I begged my parents to find you and tell you about her, because I just knew once you saw her, you'd come back to us and stay for good." She shook her head furiously, making the tears splash wildly down her cheeks. "But you never came."

Realization hit him like a thunderclap.

She didn't know.

His sternum felt cracked and his heart bled through, leaking from his chest as he ached.

He licked his lips a few times, trying to control his raging emotions. Sinking on the arm rest of his sofa, he grated out the question, "What did your parents tell you when you begged them to find me?"

Her eyebrows crinkled with confusion. She sent him an odd look as if she couldn't comprehend why he was asking such an insignificant thing. "What do you mean? They said okay. Of course. I was hormonal, irrational and upset. They would've done anything to calm me down."

Or said anything, apparently.

He tipped his chin down as he kept eye contact. "They said they would find me or that they did find me?"

"They did find you. What —"

"And how did I respond?" he cut in sharply.

Tightening her jaw, she set her hand on her hip. "Don't you remember?"

"Please, Ansley," he whispered. "Just tell me. What did they say my response was when they supposedly found me?"

"Supposedly? Are you trying to accuse my parents of —"

"What did they say?" he snapped. "How did I respond to the news of my child's birth?"

Her eyes narrowed. "You needn't pull yourself all uptight like that as if you didn't do anything wrong —"

He surged to his feet and ripped a hand through his hair as he began to pace. "Oh, I know I've committed plenty of wrongs in my life. But I refuse to own up to a wrong I didn't commit. How did I react, according to your parents?"

She shook her head, looking anxious. "They . . . they didn't say. They just . . . they just said, 'we told him,' and sent me a sad look to let me know you wouldn't be coming."

He snorted. "So they couldn't even concoct a good lie for my absence, huh?"

"What're you trying to say, Ward? That they never found you and told you about Brooklyn?"

"Until the day I saw her at J. Edgar

179

Hoover High School, I had no idea you'd had a girl. I didn't know what day she was born. I didn't even know whether you gave birth to the baby or not. And if you had, I had no idea if you kept her or not. I knew nothing. No one told me anything."

She threw her head back with a disgusted breath. "Oh, boo hoo. That excuses nothing! So they couldn't find you and lied to me about it. So what? You had seventeen years to come to us and get your answers about her. But you never came."

He wiped at his face and looked away. "Believe me, if I'd known you wanted me there, I would've come as soon as I was able."

"Yet you didn't bother to find out whether or not I did want you around," she insisted.

"Ansley, I didn't come when she was born because I was in jail."

Ansley blinked, seemingly digesting that. When she opened her mouth, he continued.

"They imprisoned me for three years. For raping you."

Again, she froze, simply staring at him. Then she shook her head. "Excuse me?"

He closed his eyes and buried his face in his hands. "I thought you knew. Heaven help me, I thought you were the one who pressed the charges against me. I thought it was what you wanted. You ask me why I never came for seventeen years. It's because I thought you put me in jail for hurting you. Something like that sends a pretty clear message to a guy that you want him to stay away from you for the rest of your life and he certainly has no business anywhere near any children you might have. The only reason I dared to contact you the other day was because Brooklyn seemed to want to know me."

"This . . . this makes no sense. You went to jail? How is that even possible? Wouldn't I know? Shouldn't I know? I mean, I was the supposed victim. Wouldn't I need to be the one to file charges against you?"

"Well, technically, the state decides whether or not to file the charges. Though I think, in this case, they wouldn't have."

She frowned. "Then . . ."

He shrugged. "You were a minor. Your parents probably forced the issue in your place."

Her face turned grey. "They wouldn't," she whispered. But he could see on her face, she knew they would, knew they had.

He lowered his gaze when he admitted, "They were there. At my hearing."

"They . . ." She didn't look like she could continue. She covered her mouth with both hands and just gaped at him. "I still don't get it," she insisted, lowering her fingers. "I mean, how could I know nothing? Wouldn't . . . wouldn't they need to question me in the trial?"

"There was no trial." Ward scratched at the back of his neck and winced before confessing, "I pled guilty at the hearing, and that was that. Three years in jail."

Her eyes flamed wide. "You did what? Are you insane? Why would you do that? Why would you plead guilty?"

"Ansley . . . You were fifteen. I was a legal adult. Doesn't matter what really happened that night. It was still statutory —"

"Don't say it," she warned.

He smiled softly at her insistence to scratch that dreaded word from his vocabulary.

She wiped at her cheeks as if patting away invisible tears, then she blew out a resolute breath. "You still didn't have to plead guilty."

Ward respected her spunk. But agony filled him as he continued to watch her. Not so long ago, he thought he'd never see her again. He'd thought she never wanted him to see her again. Realizing he'd just lost seventeen years at a chance to be in her and Brooklyn's life devastated him.

"I thought you knew," he repeated. "I thought it was what you wanted. I thought you hated me and you wanted to punish me for lying to you, for hurting you, for ruining your life. And I wanted to take whatever punishment you wanted to give me. So I pled guilty."

She shook her head. "I can't believe I knew none of this."

He shrugged. "I imagine you were a bit too preoccupied having a baby. Plus, I'm sure you parents wanted to protect you from it."

She barked out a harsh laugh. "And all this time I thought they'd only put out a restraining order against you?"

"If it makes you feel any better, I got one of those too."

"You did?" She lifted her face as it filled with dismay.

He nodded. "Yeah. I actually, uh, I broke it. That last time I went to see you, you know, when I was high and I scared the crap out of you on your way home from school. I'd just gotten it the day before. So . . . I was arrested for breaking my PFA, and that's when your parents pressed the rape issue."

"Ward, I am so, so sorry. If I'd known —"

He laughed. "You're kidding, right?"

She buried her red cheeks in her hands. "I know," she wailed. "I'll never be able to make it up to you."

He grasped her wrists and manually eased her fingers from her face. With a soft smile, he said, "You have absolutely nothing to apologize for."

Tears flooded her eyes. "But —"

"Stop it," he whispered harshly. "You did nothing wrong. I'm actually ecstatic to learn you didn't hate me so much that you'd sent me to jail."

He pulled her to his chest, enveloping her in his arms and tucking her face against his shoulder. She sobbed and wrapped her hands around his back, wadding a fistful of his shirt.

They held each other tight, so tight he could scarcely breathe. Her tears soaked through his shirt and seemed to saturate his very soul. He patted her hair helplessly.

"I wish . . ." She hiccupped another dry sob. "I wish this hadn't happened to us."

"Me too." He kissed her hair and caught the familiar smell in her light tresses. She still used the same shampoo. Squeezing his eyes closed, he kissed her hair again.

She clung to him, her arms hooked around him as if she never wanted to let go. He knew he didn't.

"Ward?"

"Hmm?" This time his pressed his mouth to her damp cheek.

She lifted her face from his shoulder and looked up at him. When their gazes caught, he knew. She still felt the same immediate punch of chemistry he did. Like an iron to a board, heat steamed between their sealed bodies. He suddenly felt every inch of her.

"I can't tell him," she whispered.

He blinked. "What?"

"Preston," she said. "I can't even tell Preston I'll marry him. In my head, I know it's the smart, safe, secure decision, but I just can't wrap my heart around it. It feels so wrong. I just keep asking for more time to think about it. And he keeps pressing me to say yes."

Mind reeling, Ward dropped his arms from around her and took a step back.

"When . . ." He licked his lips and told himself not to ask even as he asked, "When did he ask?"

She lifted guilty eyes, "The evening my daughter came home from school and told me about this amazing man she'd met at school named Ward Gemmell."

He swallowed.

"The thing is," she continued. "I kept waiting to feel that crazy breathless, giddy anticipation whenever I saw him. When I was fifteen, I always felt that when I was about to see you. But . . . it never came with him."

He sniffed out a sad sigh. "Yeah, I never felt that for anyone else again either."

She lifted her face and stared at him with her large brown eyes. "What do you think it means?"

With a shrug, he looked away. Gazing at her was too dangerous. It made him want to act. "I don't know. Maybe that we were young."

"Well, that's a depressing thought. Only the young get to experience such an overwhelming sensation?"

He lifted his face to find her looking at him with an expression that consumed him, filled him with a crazy breathless giddy anticipation. His lips quirked into a grin. "Yeah, it was pretty overwhelming, wasn't it?"

She stepped closer and his heart rate jacked into dangerous territory. "But the thing is," she whispered. "I'm feeling that exact same sensation right now. And I'm no longer a fifteen-year-old girl."

He exhaled. Temptation lured. No woman had ever drawn him the way Ansley Marlow did. Resisting her had never been an option.

She wetted her lips with her tongue, and he was a goner. Needing to experience every detail of the moment in every way possible, he cupped her face, reveling in the feel of her warm, smooth flesh against his palms.

He whispered her name.

She smiled and strained toward him.

His eyelashes slid closed as he tipped his face down and knew she'd turned hers up. Her breath brushed against his chin.

And someone pounded on his front door.

CHAPTER THIRTEEN

As Ward yanked guiltily away from her to answer the door, Ansley grabbed her hair in both hands, tempted to pull out all her overwhelming feelings.

She'd almost kissed him!

Body still buzzing from the sensations swirling inside her, she wanted to yell at whoever was at the door to go away. She hadn't kissed Ward in seventeen years, hadn't been close to him, inhaled his scent, seen his blue eyes sparkle with longing. The frustration of that getting cut short was more than she could bear.

Then again, she wanted to hug whoever was at the door for cutting their kiss short. What was she thinking, kissing Ward Gemmell? She didn't know him. And even when she thought she'd known him, she hadn't known him then either. The man was a stranger, and she'd just thrown herself at him.

How utterly embarrassing.

When he pulled the door open, she tensed braced for anything. The grinning teen holding a pizza made her pause.

"Hey, Ward, man. We confiscated your pizza." He strolled into the apartment, past Ward, until he saw her standing in the middle of the living room.

The two of them were so busy staring at each other, Ansley didn't see who had come in with him until she said, "Mom?"

Swerving toward the doorway, where Brooklyn stood next to a scowling Ward, Ansley's mouth dropped open. "What? How . . . ?" She cast the pizza boy a suspicious glance. "Who?"

"When you disappeared this evening, I knew you'd gone to see Ward, so . . ." Brooklyn sent her a guilty little smile. "I thought I should be there too."

Jaw tight, Ward seared the boy an expectant look, lifting one eyebrow.

"Hey, she showed up alone at Danny's Haven, looking for you." The kid shrugged and sunk a step away from Ward as Ward's face darkened. "Since I knew where you lived, I volunteered to bring her here. To you."

"Oh, you're from Danny's Haven too?" Ansley began to smile at the boy before it struck her that he was way too young to be a counselor. And if he wasn't a counselor, then he must be a troubled drug addict trying to come clean.

Realizing her daughter had just been alone with him for however long, she swung around to chastise Brooklyn, but was surprised to find Ward already pinning her with an arch look.

"What were you thinking?" he demanded. "Leaving a drug clinic alone with someone you didn't even know?"

Brooklyn's eyes grew wide. "I . . . I . . . but I saw you with him the last time I was there. Plus he said you guys were friends."

Cupping his head in both hands, Ward closed his eyes a second before answering, "I befriend every teen that comes to the clinic, Brooklyn. That doesn't mean any of them are safe for you to be around."

"Hey," pizza boy said, clearly insulted.

"You were very lucky Jace is a special case and fairly trustworthy," Ward kept talking.

"Fairly?" Jace echoed, still apparently not soothed by Ward's words.

"But I don't want you to ever take that risk again. In fact, you going to Danny's Haven alone is pretty much off the table from now on out."

Ansley lifted her eyebrows, actually a little

impressed by Ward's lecture. She'd stopped herself with the initial impulse to step in when someone started chastising her daughter, but he handled it so smoothly, she was actually tempted to pull out a pen and pad of paper to take a few notes.

Brooklyn cowered in front of her dad, gaping at him in intimidation. Then she blinked and straightened. A hopeful twinkle entered her eyes as she jerked a look toward Ansley and turned right back to Ward. "So . . . does that mean my going to Danny's Haven not-alone is okay?"

Ward opened his mouth to respond, but stopped suddenly. He glanced at Ansley, then Jace. His scowl returned.

"Hey, Jace, buddy. Thanks for taking care of Brooklyn and escorting her here." His dark frown seemed to add, now stay away from her as he took the boy's arm and propelled him to the still-open doorway. "Why don't you take this pizza with you?"

"But —"

"Here's twenty bucks to pay you back for buying it." Ward slapped the bill on top of the pizza and pressed the box against Jace's chest, nudging him backward into the hall. "I'll see you tomorrow, okay?"

He let go of the pizza so quickly Jace had to scramble to catch it. Jace's face was a mask of surprise as Ward shut the door on him, barring him from the apartment.

Actually charmed by his overprotective caveman father behavior, Ansley snickered under her breath. She shared a look with her daughter and they both seemed to read each other's thoughts. Ward turned around and paused when he caught them grinning at each other.

"What?"

Realizing this was the very first moment the three of them had ever been together, Ansley swallowed, her smile faltering. She'd dreamed of this so many times, wished for it despite how much she knew she shouldn't. And here it was. They were so close to becoming a family, and yet so far away.

As if feeling the tension beginning between them, Brooklyn twisted her hands. "So?" she asked.

Ward yanked his gaze away from Ansley and blew out an exhausted breath. "So . . ." he said. "I think your mom is okay with letting us get to know each other."

When her daughter whirled toward her, her eyes alight with joy, Ansley knew she'd made the right decision.

"For real?" Brooklyn demanded.

Ansley rolled her eyes to disguise how delighted she was as well. "For real."

"So do we, like, set up visiting rights now, or something?"

"Uh . . ." Ward scratched his head, looking uncomfortable. "I don't . . . that's probably not necessary. I mean, you don't actually want to spend every other weekend . . . here. Unless you just wanted to." His attention veered to Ansley, his expression a bit panicked before he turned back to Brooklyn. "Do you?"

Brooklyn opened her mouth, but didn't seem to know how to answer. None of them seemed to know where to go from here.

"How about we start with daily visits, set up a schedule that works for both of you, and go from there?" Ansley suggested.

Brooklyn gnawed on the corner of her lip, looking hesitant. "Daily visits for all three of us?" she asked.

"Oh, I don't —" Ansley started, unable to think up a reason why she should be involved in their father-daughter, get-to-know-each-other visits.

But Ward was already nodding. "Whatever you want," he told Brooklyn. "I'll agree to pretty much anything."

Ansley bit the inside of her lip when Brooklyn cocked her a questioning look, as if waiting for her mother's final vote on the matter. Ansley was as excited about the idea as she was panicked. She'd love to find out what the real Ward Gemmell was like these days, but she was also afraid to find out. He got under her skin a little too easily. Besides, she didn't want to interfere in what was obviously none of her business.

"Let's go ice skating," Brooklyn broke in, vibrating with excitement.

"Ice skating?" Ward looked skeptical. "I've never been ice skating. Have you?"

Ansley knew exactly how much her daughter downplayed her answer when she shrugged nonchalantly and mumbled, "A couple times." She must want to wow him with her talent.

Ward, thank goodness, didn't argue. He merely smiled the same smile that Ansley had fallen for seventeen years ago. "Ice skating it is, then. When do you two want to go?"

"Tomorrow morning," Brooklyn answered immediately without checking with Ansley first.

Ward glanced at her, though, blinking his surprise. Ansley shrugged as if she'd been helplessly swept along into Brooklyn's plans.

"Uh, well." Ward paused to scratch his scalp. "I have to work tomorrow."

Brooklyn's face lost some of its enthusiasm. "And you don't have any vacation days?"

"Well, yeah." He looked uncomfortable again. "But I've never missed work without being on death's doorstep before. I don't know . . ." He gave an uneasy laugh. "I don't want to be a bad influence on you guys the very day you decide I'm okay to have around."

"Nonsense." Brooklyn waved his worries aside. "Besides, wouldn't Mom and I be the bad influence in this instance since we're the ones who'll be taking you away from your job when you've never played hooky before?"

"So . . . you don't have school? And you don't have work?" He turned to Ansley and cast her a curious glance.

"I'm a loan officer at the bank over on Eighth and Hershel Avenue," she said. "But I could call in tomorrow."

He studied her for a moment before a grin split his face. "A banker, huh. Are you really? I can so see that."

Ansley's smile fell, not sure if she should be offended or complimented. "Why?"

He shrugged, still looking amused. "I just remember how you used to complain about the cashier in the fast food place where we'd go for our drinks, and how he was so slow about counting back my change. If he gave me a penny too much or not enough back, you always caught him on it."

She straightened her back. "I wouldn't call it complaining exactly," she hedged.

"Okay, fine. We'll say you noticed his deficiency . . . and then commented on it every time we went there."

She frowned. "Not every time."

Ward laughed. "Yes. Every time."

"Well, he was so slow. I swore the ice would melt in my drink by the time that kid doled out the change." And back then, she'd been so anxious to slide into a booth seat across from Ward and just . . . talk to him, look at him, occasionally reach her hand across the table and take his. She'd wanted nothing but to spend time with him in those days and that cashier was a time stealer.

Chuckling even harder, Ward turned to Brooklyn. "You should've seen your sweet, innocent mother. She was always nice to everyone, except that poor kid. One time she actually asked him if he needed to take his shoes off to finish counting out our change."

Her face heated. She wanted to deny his words so bad, but they were true. "I can't believe you actually just told her about that."

Brooklyn's eyebrows crinkled. "Shoes?"

she asked, looking puzzled.

"You know," Ward said, waving a hand, "that saying about counting on your fingers and toes."

Finally catching on, Brooklyn whirled to gape at Ansley, her mouth dropping open and eyes going wide. "You did not!" She sounded so scandalized. Then she covered her mouth and blurted out a tickled titter. "Mom, that was rude."

Setting her hands on her hips, Ansley whirled to scowl at Ward. "Are you going to tell her every bad thing I ever did?"

Eyes glittering with joy, he only smiled. "I think I just did. Besides, that wasn't bad. It was hilarious. And you did eventually take the time to teach him how to count out change better, did you not?"

Thrilled, yet uneasy about recounting that specific time of her life, she folded her arms over her chest and shot him a veiled look, so he wouldn't know how secretly pleased she was by his account. "I can't believe you remember all that."

Lips falling from their beautiful grin, he gazed at her with feeling as he murmured, "I remember everything about you."

She gulped. Ansley remembered everything about him too. Vivid details had come back to haunt her over the years, striking at the oddest times, rousing her when she was happy so she would realize she could be happier, and also coming when she was sad, brightening her with pleasant memories. She'd felt almost haunted by how often she would recall little things about him, wanting to escape them just as much as she had wanted to cling to them.

Next to her, Brooklyn drew in an audible breath, making Ansley blush. She jerked her attention from Ward and focused on her daughter.

Ward cleared his throat. "So . . ." he stalled. "You have school tomorrow, plus your mother and I both have to work, yet you still want to go ice-skating, huh? Why can't we just go in the evening?"

Brooklyn burrowed her brow. "Because, this is the first opportunity I have to spend with my father . . . ever. I want an entire day. Besides." She shrugged and shared a look with Ansley. "Mom gives me one day during each school year to take off, where we do pretty much whatever I want. I haven't had my day yet this year, so I want it tomorrow."

Ward looked shocked and awed. "You want to waste your one special day on me? Brooklyn, you don't have to do that. We can wait until Saturday. I usually go into Danny's Haven a couple hours on the weekends, but I don't have to this weekend. We could leave early and —"

"I don't want to wait until Saturday," Brooklyn cut him off, her face resolute.

Glancing toward Ansley, Ward lifted his eyebrows. "She's inherited your stubbornness, I see."

She merely grinned. "So is that a yes or a no?"

He studied her a moment, just enough time to make her feel warm and giddy all over. Then he shook his head slowly. "As if I could say no to either of you."

CHAPTER FOURTEEN

Ansley caught her daughter staring at her across the front seat of the car with a considering look as they drove home from Ward's apartment.

Uncomfortable under such intense scrutiny, she shifted in her seat. "What?"

Brooklyn tilted her head a little, her blue eyes full of a soft kind of wonder. "You're different around him."

Sucking in a sharp breath, Ansley drew herself up taut. "Don't be ridiculous."

But Brooklyn only snickered. "You're blushing."

Ansley huffed out a breath and turned down their street. When she went to fluff at her hair, her daughter pointed. "Oops, there's another tell. You always poof your hair when you're nervous."

Snapping her hand down, Ansley scowled. "I'm not — oh! Sometimes I wish you couldn't read me so well."

With a laugh, Brooklyn reached out and patted her arm. "Sorry, but you're just so obvious."

After a second of silence, Ansley couldn't help it any longer. She had to know. "How am I different?"

"Oh, Mom." Brooklyn looked only too happy to tease, "I'd tell you, but that would take away all the fun."

"Brooklyn Abigail Marlow," Ansley scolded. "You tell your mother what you think you know right this minute."

When her daughter answered with a tickled giggle, Ansley couldn't help it. She pulled a smiled too. She was shaking her head over the entire situation when she pulled into their drive, only to see another car parked at the curb.

"Uh oh." Brooklyn sat up straight and cast Ansley a suddenly serious look. "Looks like we're in trouble with the doctor."

Preston sat on her front steps, his arms crossed over his chest. As she parked the car, he stood and strolled toward them.

"You definitely don't have a youthful glow now," Brooklyn said, her gaze sympathetic.

Ansley knew she was right. She'd always known, but she'd fought it because it just felt wrong to accept what her heart really wanted. She hadn't been able to trust her deepest desires for years. They just didn't seem healthy.

Her parents had spent all these years pounding it into her head how Ward Gemmell was bad for her, she'd convinced herself not to search for him, not to give Brooklyn any details about him, even though her soul had cried out, always remembering, always longing.

Preston opened Ansley's driver's side door. "Everything okay?" he asked, bending down to peer inside at both ladies.

Ansley forced a cheerful smile. "Just fine. What're you doing here?"

He chuckled, stepping back and allowing her to slide from behind the wheel and exit the car. "Do I need a reason to visit my two favorite girls?"

Dusting off her shirt to iron out any wrinkles — another tell she suddenly realized she always did around the doctor so she could appear as perfect for him as possible — she offered him a tight smile. "You're too sweet to us."

When he leaned in to kiss her, she tipped her face to the side so he had to kiss her cheek. When he settled for that without any fuss or indication that he'd rather have a real kiss, guilt gnawed at her. She wouldn't have turned away like that for Ward.

Which settled one issue firmly in her mind. There was no way she could agree to marry one man when she'd just come back from almost-kissing another. Surreptitiously, she glanced across the car at Brooklyn, who lifted her eyebrows as if reading her mind.

"Where were you?" Preston asked as he looped an arm over Ansley's shoulder.

Ansley paused, not sure how to word this without upsetting him outright.

"I just met my father," Brooklyn announced with more courage than Ansley. She jutted up her chin and sent Preston a challenging look.

He narrowed his eyes and turned instantly to Ansley. "I thought we discussed this. You were going to ignore that letter."

Ansley met Preston's gaze coolly. "I told you I would handle it as I saw fit. And I feel the best thing for my daughter is for her to get to know her father."

Preston jerked his arm from around her, his face growing dark and angry, which shocked her. She'd never seen him show so much emotion before. "I can't believe this! He's a punk, Ansley. A worthless punk who's spent more than a couple years in jail for just about every crime possible. How could you be so stupid as to possibly think of letting this monster anywhere near your child?"

Her mouth worked a few times, not sure which part of his explosion to react to first.

This was the first time she'd ever seen his temper. She wasn't impressed. Frankly, she was surprised his first marriage had lasted fifteen years if he habitually called his wife stupid every time she did something he didn't approve of. And she had no idea he knew so much about Ward.

Crossing her arms over her chest, she asked, "How do you know what he's been to jail for?"

"I had a friend check his background." Preston shrugged as if that should be obvious.

Her mouth fell open. "You had him checked out? After I expressly asked you not to get involved?"

His eyebrows arched as if he couldn't believe her couth. "You asked me not to contact a lawyer. We said nothing of private detectives."

"I cannot believe you had such little faith in me to take care of my own issue."

"And with good reason." He snorted. "You apparently can't make a mature decision about this hoodlum."

"Hey, you can't talk to my mother like

that!" Appearing at Ansley's side, Brooklyn took her hand and glared daggers at Preston.

Preston sent the teen a negligent sniff and turned back to Ansley. "Once we're married, this stops."

Brooklyn opened her mouth again, but Ansley squeezed her daughter's hand to hush her. She had to pause a moment to control her temper before calmly saying, "Actually, I'm glad you brought the marriage up. And I'm glad I got to see a glimpse of this side of you. Because I see now that I could never marry you."

"But —"

She shook her head. "No. I've lived too long on my own to be dictated to as if I was a child. I think this is the first time I've done something that actually contradicted your wishes, and I don't care for the outcome."

"Neither do I, frankly. I don't appreciate my advice being ignored or my —"

Holding up a hand, she spoke over him. "I didn't ignore it. I just disagreed. And you could've handled your response with a little more decorum instead of blowing up in my face and calling me stupid."

Brooklyn's fingers tightened briefly around hers, cheering her on.

"Oh, this has nothing to do with me,

Ansley. Don't kid yourself. I didn't do anything wrong. I was the perfect, devoted, understanding beau. This is all because of that Gemmell fellow. You just came back from seeing him, so don't play the innocent with me." The loathsome sneer in his voice made her pull back, startled. "I was married fifteen years to an unfaithful trollop. I know the look of a woman who's just seen her lover."

Gasping, Ansley set her hand over her chest, outraged as well as panicked by the idea that he could see anything of the kind on her face. Was it the same thing Brooklyn had seen? Could everyone see it?

Had Ward seen it?

"My mother is not an unfaithful trollop, you big, over-bloated —"

"Brooklyn!" Letting go of the teen's fingers, Ansley nudged her in the direction of the house. "Go inside please."

"Not until he's gone," Brooklyn muttered, not budging.

Ansley pressed her fingertips to the center of her forehead. "You might as well leave, Preston. We've both posed our point of view and said what we needed to say. If all we can do from this point on is criticize, then there's no reason to continue the conversation."

Preston loomed closer, his eyes glittering with a malicious intent that spooked her, making her veer backward and tug Brooklyn slightly behind her.

"You deceived me, Ansley," he said in a soft, lethal voice. "You and your parents both. Your father made me think you were some kind of delicate lady of the manor now with your conservative, starched clothes and eloquent, graceful speech. But you're still just that little teen whore who spread her legs for the first bad boy who came sniffing around her. And you'll pay for making a fool of me. I bought you a ring! I —"

"Evening, Ansley. Brooklyn."

Together, mother and daughter jumped as the voice came from the darkened yard of their neighbor's house.

Preston spun around and peered into the dusk. "Who's out there?"

Finding her voice, Ansley had to lick her lips a few times before calling back, "Good evening, Mrs. Parnell." When she finally caught sight of the old woman standing on her front porch, she waved as any friendly neighbor would, but maybe with a little more enthusiasm than usual.

Preston huffed out a breath and lurched a step back. Without a farewell, he spun away and marched to his car. Brooklyn didn't stop cowering next to Ansley and holding her arm until he'd started the engine and pulled away from the curb.

Thinking nothing would've gotten rid of Preston faster than him realizing he had an audience for his display, Ansley turned toward her neighbor gratefully. "Thank you, Mrs. Parnell."

"Anytime, sweetie. Is that the end of that feller then?"

"I'd say so." Wishing the lady a good evening, Ansley grasped Brooklyn's hand and hurried them inside. Once the door shut, she blew out a breath. "Well. That was unpleasant."

"Oh my God." Flinging herself at Ansley, Brooklyn hugged her mother tight. "Talk about Dr. Jekyll and Mr. Hyde. I can't believe he said all that. He scared the crap out of me."

Smoothing her hands over her daughter's hair, Ansley kissed the crown of Brooklyn's head. "Well, he's gone now."

"But he said —"

"I think what he said was just bluster, sweetheart. I hurt his pride and he was upset."

Brooklyn pulled back to look up at her, her eyes wide with fear and hope. "So you don't think he'll —"

Ansley shook her head. "No. I wouldn't worry about him. Everything will be fine."

Fine or not, Mr. Hyde had definitely left an impression, though. After Brooklyn went to her room for the night, Ansley retreated to her own and went straight to her bed to sit on the corner of the mattress and stare at the wall.

The tremors finally overtook her as she sat there and shuddered. She might believe what she'd told her daughter — he'd just blustered and struck out with the intent to hurt because of his wounded pride — but he'd definitely hit his mark.

She'd been a golden child up until the moment she'd gotten pregnant. Her parents, teachers, friends, even strangers, treated her as if she could do no wrong. But afterward, all that changed. It was a brutal lesson to learn how easily a person could become a social outcast. For seventeen years, she'd tried to be as pristine as possible. Acceptable. But it only took a few well-placed barbs to set her right back on her bottom.

Wiping furiously at her eyes, she clenched her teeth, upset with herself for letting Preston get to her. She had a bright, wonderful, happy daughter, and Ward hadn't abandoned her quite the way she'd always thought he had.

And now she was free of Preston without feeling guilty about hurting him.

She should be satisfied. Instead, she felt like that pathetic no one she'd been the moment seventeen years ago when she'd revealed her pregnancy and her parents had looked at her with an expression that told her just how much she'd disappointed them.

CHAPTER FIFTEEN

"So we both agree not to tell him, right?" Ansley glanced over to gauge her daughter's reaction as Ward's truck pulled into their drive early the next morning.

"Whatever." Blue eyes stormy with unease, Brooklyn didn't glance her mother's way, merely watched her father's truck come to a complete stop.

"Brooklyn, please. There's no reason to involve him. Preston's gone now and everything is —"

"I said whatever!" Brooklyn snapped and darted away from her to race toward Ward as he stepped from the driver's side door.

Worrying her hands at her waist, Ansley watched them hug, feeling a tug of warmth at watching father and daughter unite. But she still felt uneasy about Brooklyn saying something to Ward about Preston's visit. She didn't want him to know. She didn't want him to feel responsible as if he had anything to do with her getting called a whore. And she didn't want him to step in and try to defend her, either. That's what had gotten her into this whole mess in the first place, Preston wanting to defend her against Ward and then going off the deep end when she'd rejected his help. Not that she thought Ward would go off the deep end if she rejected his help, but she didn't want to create an even bigger mess by allowing him the chance to get involved.

In other words, she wanted to protect him.

Strolling toward the hugging pair, her mind still on the evening before, she smiled softly when Ward pulled away from Brooklyn to greet Ansley with a welcoming nod. His blue eyes glittered as he glanced at her from head to toe, his gaze pausing on the skates tied together at the shoestrings and dangling over her left forearm.

"You own your own skates?"

Ansley flushed, lifting them slightly. "Oh, no. These are Brooklyn's."

He turned to his daughter, his eyebrow raised in question.

But Brooklyn simply shrugged. "Mom got them for me last Christmas."

He waited a moment as if waiting for further information, but when neither female offered any, he shrugged too. "Okay, then. Are you ladies ready to go?"

The three of them piled into his truck with Brooklyn sitting in the middle of the front bench seat. She dominated the conversation, peppering Ward all the way to the skating rink with questions about himself.

A few inquiries made him chuckle, some made him blush, but he answered every one with a good-natured grace. Hugging her seat by the door, Ansley stayed quiet, soaking in the moment and watching her daughter's fascinated face as she gazed at her father.

Letting the two go off on their own, Ansley shifted away from Ward and Brooklyn as soon as they rented him a pair of skates at the rink. As she rented her own, a smile played across her face while Brooklyn dragged him onto the ice and impatiently tried to coach Ward how to skate.

She lost track of them for a few minutes while she sat to remove her shoes and pull on the stakes. By the time she entered the rink, the pair were nowhere to be found. A split second of worry seized her with a natural intuition to worry that someone had stolen her baby — sixteen-years-old or not. Then she spotted Brooklyn in the center of the arena without her father, performing a toe jump.

Shaking her head, Ansley scanned the floor for Ward. She found him hugging the wall a second later, his legs stiff and knees unbent as he wobbled toward a mother and child gliding easily along in front of him. Trying to avoid plowing into them, he waved his arms, probably trying to slow down and ended up stumbling and falling on his rump.

Ansley laughed aloud and skated his way. "Did your instructor give up on you already?"

He looked up with an innocent but amused grin. "I think I'm a hopeless cause."

"No one's a hopeless cause." She held her hand down to him. "I think it's more like Brooklyn has never had the patience to teach anyone anything."

Taking her hand with a grateful, winded thanks, he held onto the wall as she guided him upright, their thick-gloved hands slipping once from lack of a good grip.

"Where did she go?" he asked, letting go of her to scan the rink. "She said she was going to circle a few times and come back to check on me."

Though she tried, Ansley couldn't hide her amused smile. He had looked right past Brooklyn twice already. After clearing her throat discreetly, she pointed. "She's right there."

He looked, squinted his eyes, and then frowned. "Where?"

Ansley didn't point this time. "She's the one . . . spinning."

"Spin . . ." He finally focused on his daughter. His mouth dropped open when he saw her finishing up her scratch spin. An inarticulate sound of shock emerged.

Finally, he glanced Ansley's way. "Thank goodness we weren't competing for money or anything. I think I've just been hustled."

Ansley laughed. "I have a feeling she only wanted to surprise you with her talent."

He nodded. "Consider me surprised." His attention veered back to Brooklyn as she wove a figure eight between other skaters. "I've seen Olympic ice skating on TV once or twice. I can't tell the difference between her and them."

Ansley's pride bubbled inside her. "She's been fascinated with skating since she was five. I finally let her get lessons at eight. And every time I watch her on the rink, I'm still amazed by what she can do."

"Yeah," he murmured, obviously amazed himself.

Watching his face as he watched their daughter, she forgot all about the evening

215

before and the feelings of low self-worth Preston had instilled in her.

"Come on." She hooked her arm through his, the bulky thickness of their coats muffling the feeling of being so close to him. "Let's get some hot chocolate. We can watch her from the other side of the wall and take off these skates while we're at it."

"But —"

"Trust me. She's in her zone and will be there for a while. She won't notice how early you gave up."

He blinked and wrinkled his brow. "I wouldn't call it giving up, per say."

Ansley laughed, feeling more alive than she had in a long time. "Come on."

Ward nodded and willingly let her lead him off the ice.

"Here you go."

Ansley jumped at the sound of Ward's voice behind her. She turned from watching Brooklyn working on her Axel jump and found him holding two steaming Styrofoam cups. Mouth watering for that first sip of cocoa, she grinned and held up her hands. "Thanks."

He sat beside her on the bench, and they sipped in silence, each watching Brooklyn twirl around the ice.

"She's really something else."

Ansley swelled with more pride. "Yeah."

Ward lowered his cup of cocoa to his lap and looked down into the steaming liquid before he cleared his throat. "So . . . have you, uh, talked to your parents yet, about the conversation we had last night?"

For a moment, Ansley couldn't remember what conversation he was referring to before it all came flooding back. She'd been so upset to learn how they had deceived her about Ward. She'd been ready to call them and strike out that very instant. Then she and Ward had almost kissed, Brooklyn had shown up, and they'd gone home to the scene with Preston. In between all that, she'd forgotten about how much she wanted to chew out Mom and Dad.

But now that Ward mentioned them, she remembered she had a couple more reasons to bicker at her parents. They'd been the ones to introduce her to Preston. He'd been a fellow doctor at the same hospital where her father practiced. Her mother had invited both her and him to dinner on the same evening so they could meet.

"You really shouldn't be so upset with them." Ward touched her elbow briefly before pulling away. "All they did was love you and try to protect you as best as they could. Not every decision a person makes is always the right one, but I know for certain they only had your best interest at heart. And a little forgiveness from the most important people in your life goes a long way." He looked at her meaningfully.

Ansley swallowed, realizing what he was truly asking. "You know, I've forgiven you for leaving, right?" After learning what she'd learned last night, how could she not?

He shuddered out a breath and drained the rest of his cocoa. "I don't deserve it," he murmured into the empty cup.

She blew out a breath. "Well, neither do my parents in my opinion but you still want me to forgive them, don't you?"

He shook his head and sent her an almost warning look. "I hate it when my own advice is used against me." Then he grinned. But as soon as his gaze met hers, his smile dropped. "You wouldn't believe how many times I wanted to look you up over the years, curious about how you were doing, wondering about the baby." He glanced toward the rink, found Brooklyn immediately, and his gaze softened. "I just wanted to apologize . . . for everything."

Mouth going dry, Ansley took a quick sip. "So why didn't you?"

"Well, there was the whole restraining

order thing, then the going to jail for rape thing. I didn't think you wanted me anywhere near you. I was afraid you'd call the police and I'd end up in jail for coming within a hundred feet of you. And then there was the fact I did go visit my mom after I cleaned up. I wanted to apologize to her for being such a handful in my teen years and hopefully somehow make amends. But she slammed the door in my face."

Ansley covered his gloved hand with her own. "Oh, Ward. That's awful."

"I figured if my own mother couldn't forgive me for being what I was, then you certainly wouldn't."

"I'm so sorry. I can't even imagine scorning my own child like that."

He began to play with her glove, tugging at the fingers. "One of her daughters answered the door. My half-sister. I thought she was the older one, but so much time had passed, I found out she was actually the younger one. I felt like such a loser, not even knowing which sister I was looking at. Then my mom came to the door and when she started screaming at me, my sister crouched down behind her, looking at me as if I was the devil."

When he slid her glove off her hand completely, a mischievous smile lit his face.

Reading his expression, Ansley gasped and dove forward to retrieve her glove. He laughed and held it out away from her so she had to lean across him to grasp it. Once she wrapped her bare fingers around the knitted cotton, her gaze sought his. She sucked in a breath when she realized how close their faces were. When she ripped the glove from his hand, he let her take it without a word.

Clearing her throat, she straightened and flushed, staring straight ahead at the rink, but seeing nothing.

Ward cleared his throat and began to play with his own gloves, slipping them slowly off his hands. "She sent me an invitation last year. My younger sister. She invited me to her wedding. But, yeah. I didn't go. Figured it was a pity invite anyway."

Ansley glanced down at his bare hands as he folded and refolded the gloves. Reaching out, she covered his warm fingers with her own. Bare skin to bare skin. "You should've gone."

Lifting his attention even as he threaded his fingers through hers and held on, he sent her a small smile. "That's not what you're supposed to tell me. You're supposed to tell me I made the right choice."

She shook her head. "Sorry. But I prefer

honesty."

He chuckled. "That's what I always loved about you." Lifting their interlaced fingers to his mouth, he pressed a simple, warm kiss to her knuckles. "Honest Ansley." When he looked at her, he was still grinning.

But he must've read the expression on her face. She had no idea what she looked like, she only knew how she felt. Stunned, hopeful, flabbergasted, hopeful. Had she mentioned hopeful?

Smile dropping flat, he let go of her hand, "I mean . . ." He shook his head. His lips moved as he tried to come up with a way to backtrack when Brooklyn appeared in front of them, bringing a wave of fresh, cold air with her as she skidded to a stop in front of them.

"Did anyone save some cocoa for me?" She plopped down on the bench next to Ward and caught her breath as she brushed wind-tossed dark hair out of her face.

Ansley silently passed over her half-finished drink, briefly crossing her arm across Ward. As her daughter gulped without grace, he bumped his knee into hers. "Hey, Little Miss Trickster, you, making me think you hardly ever skated. You were amazing out there on that ice."

Brooklyn glowed as she lowered the cup

and then swiped the back of her hand over her cocoa mustache. "Did you really think so?"

He snorted. "I think I'm going to start saving up money now so I can buy a ticket to the next winter Olympics because no way am I going to miss watching you get a gold medal live."

Ducking her head as she blushed, she tucked a piece of hair behind her ear and mumbled, "I'm not quite that good yet. I can't even do a Double Axel yet."

Ward rolled his eyes Ansley's way, sharing a look with her, before turning back to their daughter. "I have no clue what a Double Axel is, but I bet you'll nail it in no time."

"Yeah," Brooklyn wasn't too shy to admit. "Maybe."

With a laugh, Ward reached out, one hand grasping Brooklyn's, his other taking hold of Ansley's fingers. "Come on, you two. I'm starving. Let's find something to eat around here. My treat."

CHAPTER SIXTEEN

Seated in the middle of the bench seat of Ward's truck, Brooklyn leaned forward to turn up the song on the radio. He could tell she was happy when she began to sing along to the words and bebop her head back and forth.

Sharing a grin with Ansley across the cab of his truck, he slowed to turn the corner, and didn't speed up again, wanting to stretch his time with both of them as long as possible. Today had been one of the nicest days of his life. And as dusk gathered, so did a measure of panic.

He didn't want to give them up yet and drop them off at their house, only to drive off to his cold, lonely apartment. He wanted to keep them both and never let go. But he knew it'd be a long while before he could work himself back into such a hallowed position. He'd get there though, someday, because he wasn't giving up until he did.

He wanted to be a permanent aspect in both their lives.

A pause in Brooklyn's contented singing jarred him from his thoughts. Catching the uneasy look on her face, he asked, "What's wrong?"

She pointed to the car parked in front of her and Ansley's house. "Grandma and Grandpa are here."

Ansley sat up straighter and cringed when she saw the car. Lowering the volume of the song on the radio, Ward pulled into the drive and parked behind Ansley's car. "Mind if I walk you ladies to the door?" he asked, not really giving them an option as he pushed from the truck and came around to meet them on the passenger side as they alighted.

"You don't have to stick around," Ansley told him, though he noted a certain look in her eyes, something vulnerable and pleading, actually begging him to stay. "It's never pretty when my parents visit."

"Yeah, because they spend the whole time degrading you for something or other," Brooklyn muttered as she started for the house.

Ward trailed behind, walking beside Ansley. "I take it they have a key to the place."

She sent him a disgusted look. "They

insisted on it when I had to ask them to co-sign on my house loan."

He nodded but didn't comment. The front door opened just as Brooklyn reached it. Mrs. Marlow hadn't changed much in the past seventeen years. She still wore her hair the same, and looked the same age. But as well pickled in vinegar as she was, he wasn't all that surprised.

She tugged her granddaughter into the house for a hug. Relieved Ansley's parents didn't treat Brooklyn unacceptably because of her origins, he reached out and briefly squeezed the hand of the woman beside him before letting go. Ansley glanced up at him, her turmoil swirling in her gaze before she turned away and stepped inside. He followed, quietly shutting the door behind him.

But he might as well have slammed it. Mrs. Marlow jumped as it closed, whirling toward him to gape. A second later, her face darkened. "So it's true. You threw Preston over for the drug addict."

Ward drew in a quiet breath, refusing to react as Ansley's father appeared in the opening to the kitchen.

"We expected better from you than this, Ansley."

Ansley kept her composure as she smoothed down the front of her shirt. "I see

Preston has spoken to you already."

"Yes, he has." Her mother let go of Brooklyn to approach Ansley. "And he told us you'd called off the wedding. My God, Ansley. What are you —"

"I didn't call off the wedding." Ansley straightened her back and stiffened her shoulders. "There never was a wedding to begin with, because I never told him I'd marry him. I was thinking about it. Last night, I simply made my final decision and said no."

She had? Ward sucked in a breath. When he gained everyone's attention, he opened his mouth, but no words came.

Why had she told her doctor no to marriage last night . . . right after almost kissing him? He didn't dare to hope.

"You will not believe some of the things Preston told us about you, Ansley," her father said, his voice reprimanding. Disapproving.

"Did he tell you what he said to her?" Brooklyn asked, her hands fisted down at her sides, and her eyes flaring with anger. "Did he tell you what he called her?"

Neither of her grandparents looked too interested in what Ansley's near-fiancé had called her, but Ward sure was. Lifting his eyebrows, Ward asked in a low voice, "What did he call her?"

Brooklyn opened her mouth but froze when she caught a stern look from her mother. Ward hardened his jaw, realizing it must've been bad if Ansley didn't want him to know. That's okay, he'd ferret out the truth later.

For now, he stuck by Ansley's side as it remained obvious her parents weren't going to relent any time soon.

"My God, Ansley, this is your father's colleague. Do you still have no care for his reputation at all?"

Ward scowled and opened his mouth. The Ansley he knew would never do anything to risk the reputation of one of her loved ones.

But Mr. Marlow exploded, "For God's sake. He bought you a ring!"

Ansley shook her head, looking flabbergasted. "Well, I certainly didn't ask him to."

"And we didn't ask for a daughter who got pregnant at fifteen, but we've learned to deal with it. Is it too much to expect you to do this for us, help us save a little face after the embarrassment you put us through?"

Brooklyn looked like she was about to defend her mother again, which warmed Ward even more. But this time, he was the one to hush her. Setting a hand on her shoulder, he glared at Dr. and Mrs. Marlow.

"I think you're crossing the line," he said, using everything in his power to keep his boiling temper out of his voice. "What happened when she was fifteen was not her fault. And even if it was, Ansley doesn't owe you anything, and she certainly shouldn't have to marry someone just to help you save some kind of face."

Mrs. Marlow merely stiffened her shoulders with righteous indignation, and stared down her haughty nose at him. "What are you even doing here?"

Ansley grabbed his arm as if keeping him by her side, when really, he wasn't budging from her side unless she pushed him away. "He's here because Brooklyn and I want him here."

With a hearty nod, Brooklyn agreed, stepping backward so she was standing on the other side of him. His chest swelled at their loyalty. Never in a million years had he imagined that Ansley, or her daughter, would feel an ounce of loyalty toward him. Not after what he'd put them through, and certainly not after what his reappearance in their life was putting them through now.

"And he probably would've been here for the past seventeen years," Ansley hissed, "if you two hadn't sent him to jail!"

Brooklyn spun to face her mother. "What?"

Jabbing her finger at her parents, Ansley announced, "They made sure your father spent three years in jail for . . . hurting me. Which was a total lie. Then, on the day you were born, I asked them to tell him about you. And they didn't, lying again, when they said they had."

Mrs. Marlow sniffed and rolled her eyes. "My God, Ansley. The boy was a filthy, worthless hoodlum. What did you expect us to do?"

Brooklyn gasped. "So it's true. You're the ones who kept him away from me my whole life?"

Growling out a sound of frustrated outrage, Ansley's mother stomped her foot before whirling to nail Ward with an icy glare. "Are you satisfied with yourself? Pitting our only daughter and grandchild against us?"

Ward shook his head sadly. "Actually, I was on your side until this evening. I assumed you had done whatever you thought was best for Ansley when she was fifteen. I couldn't hate you for protecting her. And if keeping her away from me was what was best for her, then I fully applauded your efforts. But from the way you're treating her right now, it doesn't appear to me you have her best interest at heart at all. You gave her more respect and freedom than this when she was in high school."

"That's because we learned she can't be trusted to take care of herself."

Ward snorted out an incredulous laugh. "I'm sorry, but I just spent the entire day in her company, and she is still the most amazingly honest, responsible person I know. Her daughter is definitely the most adjusted teen I know, and I'm around teenagers all day at work." Lifting his arms and glancing around the living room, he added, "This house is probably in better condition than any house I've been in, and her car looks clean with the tires in good condition. I mean, honestly, what part of any of that makes you think she's not taking care of herself, or her daughter, or her entire life?"

When neither of her parents had a ready answer, he felt the need to push a little more. "And from what I can tell, she's had to do all this by herself because you two have been too busy dictating to her these past seventeen years to actually help her where she really needed the help because you've been too concerned with your own reputations."

Folding his arms over his chest, Mr. Marlow arched a brow. "Do you really feel as if you're in a position to tell us what we haven't done for Ansley and Brooklyn these past seventeen years?"

"Enough!" Ansley yelled above everyone. Waving her hands, she glared at her parents. "I don't feel like talking to either of you at the moment. Since Ward is right, and I do pay all the mortgage on this house, I'm claiming ownership of it. And I want you both gone when I come back into this room."

Turning away from them, she kept her head held high as she strode down the hall.

Awed as he watched her go, the regal set of her shoulders both stubborn and elegant, Ward slowly turned back to Ansley's parents. When Brooklyn laced her arm through his, siding with him, he felt encouraged.

"If it's any consolation," he started calmly, "I understand why you lied to her, why you kept my imprisonment from her. You were just being over-protective parents. But she feels wronged right now and she has plenty of reason to feel that way. So you need to take that into consideration. And you need to leave as she asked you to do."

He wasn't sure why they bought his bluff. If they'd been determined to stay, he wouldn't have bodily removed them. They were Ansley's parents. Brooklyn's grandparents. But they sniffed at him, lifting their noses as if offended, and picked their way to the exit.

Finally exhaling when the front door closed after them, he turned to Brooklyn. She looked as rattled as he felt, her eyes wide and cheeks flushed.

Impulsively hugging her to his side, he kissed her hair. "You okay?"

She nodded against him, clinging to his arm. "Yeah. I just . . . after tonight and last night, I think this is the most drama this house has ever seen."

Ward frowned slightly. "They were here last night, too?"

"No. Dr. Jackson was though. He was waiting for us when we got back from your house. And when she told him she wouldn't marry him —"

"Wait." Ward caught Brooklyn's arm, squeezing it in his excitement. "She really told him she wouldn't marry him?"

His daughter's smile was a little too knowing. "Yes." Then her grin dropped as soon as it had started. "And he got really mad and told her she'd pay for embarrassing him like that and leading him on. Then he called her an unfaithful trollop. And a whore."

The rage that seized him was surreal. He wanted to find Dr. Jackson that very moment and pick him up with one hand, then squeeze until the dead man turned red in the face and stopped flailing.

"Oh, he did, did he?" he said, his jaw tight as he watched Brooklyn bob her head vigorously.

"And this guy's name is Jackson?" he asked, lifting an eyebrow.

"Yes." Brooklyn grinned again, looking happy as if she relished telling Ward the dead man's name. "Dr. Preston B. Jackson."

Ward nodded, soaking that information away in his brain. He was going to have to do a little homework to learn what he could do about Dr. Preston B. Jackson.

"So what are you going to do to him?" Brooklyn demanded, watching him a little too closely.

He snorted, forcing the fury off his face. "Nothing," he said, but he couldn't help himself. He added, "Nothing illegal anyway." Then he sighed at his own lack of self-control. "Brooklyn, I want you to know your mother isn't any of those things he called her. She never was, and she never could be even if she tried. She is, honestly, the most perfect person I've ever known. And you should be proud to have an amazing mother like her."

Blinking back a couple tears, his daughter wiped at her face and grinned. "Oh, I know. And I am." She shoved lightly on his arm. "So, are you going to go check on her or not?"

He stumbled a step away at her prodding, alarmed. "I don't . . . do you think I should?"

Brooklyn rolled her eyes. "Yes! So get going already."

Pausing before he raced in the direction Ansley had gone, he grinned at the girl before him. "And just so you know. I'm really proud to have a daughter like you. When you stood up for her tonight, I was honored to be your father. And I'm going to spend the rest of my life attempting to be worthy of an amazing person like you."

"Oh my God." Brooklyn wiped at her wet cheeks. "You better really go now before I'm a mushy pile of blubber."

Ward grinned and gave her another quick, crushing hug. "I know I just met you. But I already love you with my whole heart, kiddo. I can't believe I was lucky enough to find a way into your life."

Before she could respond, he pressed another smacking kiss to her hair and hurried down the very hallway Ansley had escaped.

CHAPTER SEVENTEEN

Ansley stood in her bathroom, internally debating with herself when the partially closed door behind her opened a few inches as someone tapped on it.

"Ansley?"

"I'm okay, I just . . ."

The door slowly swung open more to reveal Ward, the mask of concern on his face more than she could take. Shoulders slumping, she lifted the bottle in her hand and gave a humorless laugh. "I hate taking these things."

He studied her a moment, then reached out and slowly took the prescription from her. Without reading the label, he kept his gaze on her as he set it back in the cupboard. "Then don't."

"But they're for my headaches, and I really need one right now."

He just smiled. "How about you let me try a few home remedies on you first. I've helped some of my teens deal with head-aches the natural way before."

She'd try anything to keep from taking a pill. So she closed her eyes and nodded, feeling defeated. When Ward's gentle hands cradled her shoulders, she followed where he led, directing her back into her bedroom.

"Let's keep it dark in here." Keeping the bath light on, he nudged open the door so it sprayed a muted glow over her bed before he killed the overhead in her bedroom. "The best thing for you right now is darkness and relaxation." He took her hand, his fingers warm and more relaxing than anything she'd encountered in months, maybe years.

When he led her toward her bed, she followed without resistance. After coaxing her to lie on her back, he sat on the edge of the mattress by her hip and still holding her hand, brought her own fingers up to her nose.

"Squeeze the hard cartilage part and don't let go for a couple minutes. Let's see if we can pinch some of the pressure out of there."

She nodded and tried squeezing the bridge of her own nose.

"Brooklyn?" Ward called as he rubbed Ansley's shoulder.

Their daughter appeared in the doorway

almost immediately. When she saw Ansley on the bed, her legs sprawled out in front of her with Ward plumping her pillows behind her head, she jerked to an abrupt halt. "What's wrong?"

"Your mom has a headache."

"Again?" Sounding incredulous, she charged into the room, meeting Ansley's gaze with concern wrinkling her brow. "Do you want me to get your pills?"

"No," Ward answered for her. "We're going to try a couple different things first. Could you do me a favor?"

"Sure. What do you need?" She skipped around to sit at Ansley's other side so she could slowly rub her mother's arm. It made Ansley's emotions soften to see her daughter being so compassionate.

"First, find two small hand towels and toss them into the freezer for a couple of minutes. When they're cool, we're going to drape one over her eyes and roll one up under her neck. Meanwhile, see if there is any pickle juice and black cumin in the kitchen."

Brooklyn wrinkled her nose. "Black cumin?" she asked just as Ansley started to sit up and said, "Pickle juice?"

Ward calmly put a hand on her arm and eased her back down. "The pickle juice is for dehydration. You didn't drink much all day, so we need to get some sodium and liquids down you in case that's helping cause the headache. The oils in black cumin are just some cure-all I've heard about over the years." He shrugged. "Can't hurt to try it."

He glanced expectantly at Brooklyn, who popped to her feet and disappeared from the room.

"Until we get all that, why don't you close your eyes and just find your happy place."

She gurgled out a surprised laugh. "My happy place?"

He shrugged, sending her a rueful grin. "Sure. Don't you have one?"

Blushing and feeling silly for even thinking about such a thing, she shrugged. "I . . . I don't know. I've never thought about it before."

"Well, there's half your problem. When things get stressful, you need something to help relax you. To ground you. From all my counseling training, I've learned the best thing you could do at a time like this is close your eyes and think up happy thoughts or remember happy memories."

"Okay," she closed her eyes and was transported.

"Got it?" he asked into her ear.

She nodded and opened her eyes. "Where's your happy place?" she whispered.

His grin was flirtatious, his blue eyes sparkling with mischief. "You tell me about yours, I'll tell you about mine."

She flushed. "I was remembering when Brooklyn was born. My parents had left the hospital for the night and the nurse had just come in to check on us. It was our first moment totally alone. She was sleeping in my arms and all I could do was just stare at her. She was so precious. And all mine."

"That's amazing," he whispered. "I . . ." Looking uncertain, he rubbed at the back of his neck before sending her a sad smile. "I wish I could've been there to share that with you, though I guess the magic part of it was probably that you actually got to be alone with her."

She wanted to tell him it would've been even more magical if he'd been there. But she was tired of boo-hooing over past regrets. She wanted to move forward.

Patting his knee, she said, "Now your turn."

He cleared his throat and glanced away. "It's nothing so special," he mumbled, looking embarrassed.

Ansley arched an eyebrow. "Too bad. I told you mine. Now you have to share."

He rolled his eyes and relented. "Okay, it . . . it's hummingbirds. Strange, I know."

"Hummingbirds?" She crinkled her brow and tried to tell herself she wasn't disappointed. He hadn't been part of her happy place, why had she thought she'd have any part of his? But hummingbirds? Really?

He nodded and glanced down at his hands. "Yeah. I, uh, I always equated you to a hummingbird for some reason. So small yet mighty, full of life and color and movement. Whenever you were around, you were the only thing I could see. As the years passed and your face began to blur in my head, I'd just picture hummingbirds and that always calmed me down."

The breath rushed from her lungs as she stared at him. Her body had been in an uproar of frazzled, over sensitized nerves since the moment her daughter had come home and said his name. But this sent them over the edge.

Stupid or illogical, she didn't care. She loved this man, the one sitting on her bed, trying to ease her headache and confessing what his happy place was.

She opened her mouth, probably to tell him so too, but Brooklyn breezed into the room.

"Got it," she announced, looking proud of

241

herself and eager to help.

"Ah, perfect." Ward accepted the supplies. After turning back to Ansley, he had her sit up as he crushed the cumin into a napkin with the flat of a spoon Brooklyn had also brought in.

"If you go to an herbal shop, you can probably buy a bottle of black seed oil, which comes from cumin. I'd say take a couple drops a day with a teaspoon of honey, and it'll help these migraines a lot."

With that, he trickled the cumin into the pickle juice. As he held it out to her, Ansley made a face. And he asked their daughter to get a cup of water to chase the flavor.

"Don't eat a lot of dairy, chocolate, eggs or coffee tomorrow, okay?" he instructed as she drained half the cup.

She shuddered at the strange flavor and choked out, "Yes, doctor." But as soon as the words crossed her lips, she straightened with a frown. "Wait. I just dated a doctor for eight months. Why didn't he suggest any of these tips?"

Ward shrugged, his face darkening as she mentioned Preston. "I don't know. Doctors usually want you to come back for repeat business though. Maybe he thought that if he gave you too much information you wouldn't need him anymore."

She frowned. Hmm. Would Preston purposely keep her in pain just so she'd feel like she needed him?

Ward handed her the water Brooklyn had gotten. As she gulped it, he asked, "Any better yet?"

Surprisingly enough, she was better. There was still small traces of pain, but it was already decreasing.

Amazing.

"Wow," she announced. "Yes, it is better. I almost feel brand new. I don't think I'll ever take another pill again."

"If that's what you want." Ward pushed to his feet and momentarily disappeared into her bathroom. When he emerged, he grinned, "There. I got rid of them for you."

Oh, yeah. It was official. As he came back to her side to sit with her and Brooklyn, she knew; she was definitely in love with Ward Gemmell. All over again.

Despite reason or logic, her heart trusted him.

CHAPTER EIGHTEEN

Preston was true to his word. Ansley hadn't heard the last of him.

Since tattling to her parents hadn't gotten him far, he tried the concerned friend approach. Calling her that Saturday, he said, "Ansley, I'm worried about you. I received a little more information about this Gemmell character. I don't want to alarm you, but . . . sweetheart he was convicted and sentenced for raping a girl. He's not safe, and you need to keep Brooklyn as far away from him as possible."

Ansley rolled her eyes. "Is that all your private detective friend found on him?"

"Darling, I know you want to believe the best of people, but this is true. He spent three years in a correctional facility for —"

"I know, Preston," Ansley cut him off. "And if your friend had done his research properly, he would know I was the reason Ward spent those three years in prison.

Because I was statutorily too young to be involved with him. Not because he brutally hurt some other girl."

Preston grew silent. Then incredulously, he said, "You were the reason?"

"Yes. Or maybe I should say my parents were the reason he was arrested."

"So, he has a thing for young girls then. Is it safe for him to work at a teen clinic?"

"Oh, don't. Just stop. Ward was barely eighteen, practically the same age I was."

"He's still not a reliable character. He was also incarcerated for public intoxication, possession of an illegal substance, vandalism, trespassing —"

"Did any of these charges happen less than fifteen years ago?"

Again, Preston didn't immediately answer. He sighed. "Ansley, don't be stupid. Just because he hasn't been arrested recently doesn't mean —"

"Well, I think it does," she broke in. "I believe some people can actually be rehabilitated. They can improve. Ward Gemmell is one of them. And even if he wasn't, I don't see how it's any of your concern. I told you I won't marry you. I don't want to date you any longer either. And frankly, I don't even want to be just friends, Preston. I'm sorry, but it's over."

"You're making a big mistake. You need me."

Need him? She wanted to laugh. Yeah, she needed a man to call her awful names as much as she needed a kick in the face.

"Really?" She lifted an eyebrow. "Is that why I feel happier and better in the days we've been apart than all eight of the months we were together? Because I need you so much? Hardly. And another thing, Preston. Those stupid pills you prescribed me are worthless. Ward flushed them down the toilet and helped me get rid of my headache without them. I don't need you at all. Please, leave me alone."

For the first time in her life, she hung up on someone.

And felt good about it.

Tempted to a do a little victory dance around her bedroom, she was still grinning at the cell phone in her hand, rather proud of herself for standing up to him, when Brooklyn strolled inside and flopped on her bed, looking depressed.

"I know we made plans to see Dad again in a couple days, but I want to see him now."

Nothing captured Ansley's attention like the mention of Brooklyn's father. And now that Brooklyn brought up the subject, she wanted to see him too.

She sat on the edge of her mattress next to her daughter and rubbed Brooklyn's back. "So he said you could call him dad, huh?"

Brooklyn lifted her face and frowned. "Well . . . no, but . . . he is my dad. Why would he care if I called him dad?"

Ansley's lips quirked. She had a feeling Ward wouldn't mind at all. She just liked how easily Brooklyn labeled him so. Confirmed that she'd made the right decision to steer clear of Dr. Jackson, Ansley slapped her daughter's backside as she stood up.

"Come on. I want to see him sooner too. Let's make some cookies and go hang out in his neighborhood so we'll have a reason to drop by."

Popping off the bed, Brooklyn was full of grins. "Now you're talking."

Ward sat on the lip of the bathtub as he watched Jace hang his head over the toilet in his bathroom and dry heave.

"I hate you so much right now, Ward."

Shaking his head, Ward merely chuckled as he focused on the screen of his iPad where he was playing Angry Birds. "Hey, I didn't tell you to quit cold turkey. You knew there would be withdrawal symptoms."

The teen panted for a second, then

reached for the roll of toilet paper he was rapidly going through so he could wipe his mouth and the perspiration dripping down his face. After tossing the used tissue, he bowed his head, closed his eyes and swayed slightly back and forth.

"So you're saying I should've kept taking drugs then?"

"No." Ward rolled his eyes. "How many times have we been over this? You don't recover by stopping it abruptly. You create a new lifestyle, wean yourself off, and make it so you don't find yourself in the situation where you need to use them again."

"Easy for you to say. You're not stuck living with my pot-selling mom for another year before you turn eighteen."

Gnashing his teeth, Ward wished with all his soul he could fix that. He wanted to take Jace out of his environment and surround him with a good, nurturing family he deserved.

"I know it's not easy," he started softly. "I've been there. And it sucks. Bad. But I have a feeling you haven't been completely honest with me, Jace. You wouldn't have shown up on my doorstep quite this sick this morning if you'd really cut down as much as you've led me to believe you have."

"So, I lied." Jace clutched the porcelain in front of him and he held his pale, drawn face over the toilet before falling back onto his haunches when nothing came up. "So, what?"

Ward relaxed, glad the vomiting had finally passed. But the racing heart and muscle tension was still going strong, he decided when Jace set his hand over his chest and rubbed a circle over his heart as he shuddered and tightened up his shoulders as if cold.

"Yeah, I can tell you lied. The question is why. You knew there was no competition to quit, there was no judgment being cast. You didn't have a deadline or anything. Why weren't you just honest with me?"

Jace sent him a rebellious scowl as he hovered against the toilet. "Because I wanted to impress you," he mumbled through chattering teeth.

Chest constricting, Ward held his breath and counted to ten. It struck him again how important his job was. He wasn't just counseling troubled kids and trying to help them kick a bad addiction. He was a role model. Some of his clients actually looked up to him and saw him as family since their own family was usually too messed up to care about them. And Jace was one of those kids.

Blown away by the fact that anyone would actually want his approval, he heaved out a breath. "Jace, you impress me every time you walk through the doors of Danny's Haven. You are one bright kid and I never once doubted you wouldn't be able to kick this habit. I still think you'll nip it in the bud. But what made you finally stop all of it, and so suddenly?"

Jace's cheeks flushed and he glanced away. "I don't know. I just wanted to be better. Worthy."

Since he'd lied to Ward about cutting down his habit before, Ward was pretty sure he hadn't stopped cold turkey to be worthy of Ward. He had another reason, something a lot more motivating and most-likely prettier than Ward.

"A girl?" he guessed, lifting one eyebrow.

Jace coughed into his hand and refused to answer.

Ward grinned. "What's her name?"

Slicing him a dirty look, the teen grumbled, "I didn't say it was because of a girl."

"Yeah, you didn't have to either." Grin settling, Ward grew serious. "Is she worth it?" he finally asked. "She's not some —"

"Yes, she's worth it," Jace snapped, his eyes narrowing as he defended his mystery girl. "She's good and honest and pure and . . . and too good to ever have anything to do with me." With a groan, he shut his eyes and let his back fall against the side of the bathtub until he was sitting next to Ward's leg. "I don't even know why I bothered. I'd never have a chance, and we're from totally different worlds. And I've only talked to her one time, and —"

Suddenly suspicious, Ward broke in, "You're not talking about Brooklyn, are you?"

Though his face was already white, Jace's features leached of color as he immediately said, "No." Then his big eyes veered Ward's way, and he winced. "Would it be totally awful if I was?"

Ward stared at him, unable to breathe. His past blared through his brain as he saw history wanting to repeat itself. But there was no way he'd ever let Brooklyn go through what her mother had. No way he'd let Jace get that close to her to hurt her.

He might be a hypocrite that way, but this was his daughter they were talking about.

The urge to strangle the seventeen-year-old must've reflected on his face because Jace pulled away from him and lifted both hands. "Hey, you know I wouldn't do anything. I'll probably never even see her again."

"Then why did she cause you to quit?" Ward asked from gritted teeth.

"She didn't," Jace insisted, only to shrug. "I mean, not really. I just . . . when I brought her over to your house the other day, I knew I'd never have a chance with a girl like her until I changed my life completely. I'm sick of living this way, Ward. I want to exist in the kind of world she exists in."

Anger deflating, Ward sighed. "You will. Someday. It's going to be hard until you can get away from home, but I'll be here for you. No matter what . . . as long as you don't touch my daughter before that. Don't even talk to her until you have a good year away from drugs under your belt."

Jace just rolled his eyes. "Geez, you've been a dad for what, a whole week now, and you already have the fatherly lecture down pat. Show off."

"Shut up." Ward sniffed out an amused smile. "But I'm still serious about what I said."

"Believe me, I know." Grin falling, Jace looked up at Ward with sad eyes. "I'd never disrespect you like that though. I know she's off-limits. I just . . ."

When he shook his head, looking depressed, Ward wanted to hug him. He shared the kid's pain on an elemental level. He'd felt the same desperation and hopelessness back when he'd first met Ansley. He'd ached to be the kind of boy good enough for her, and he knew he never would be.

He set a hand on Jace's still-trembling shoulder and hated the frailness he could feel under Jace's cotton T-shirt. Neglected and malnourished, the boy needed a better life than what he had.

"Come on. I'll fix you something to eat."

Ward pushed to his feet to lead Jace into his kitchen, but Jace shook his head and covered his stomach with his hand.

"No. I don't think I could eat right now." When he looked up, his bloodshot eyes looked beseeching. "Would you mind if I slept on your couch for a couple hours though?"

"Not at all, bud. You look like you could use a good rest."

The marks under Jace's eyes were dark and sunken.

Ward followed him from the bathroom and down a short hall into the apartment's tiny living room. When Jace collapsed onto the sofa, he was out about as soon as his cheek hit the cushions. Ward stood over him and watched him for a couple minutes, wondering how long he'd spend in jail if he went to Jace's crack-dealing mother's house right now to strangle her.

How could she do this to her own son?

He shook his head, reminding himself he wasn't a very good example of the ideal parent, and retreated to his bedroom to find another blanket. After spreading it over the sleeping teen, he settled himself into a side chair and continued the muted game on his iPad as he kept guard over the boy. Just because Jace had stopped vomiting didn't mean he was clear yet. Detoxing as abruptly as Jace had could lead to heart attack, seizure, stroke, or any number of calamities.

Ward glanced at him every time he flicked his finger across the screen. But Jace remained calm and peaceful in sleep.

About two hours into the nap, a soft knock fell on Ward's apartment door. He frowned and set his tablet aside, wondering who was visiting this time. Though it was his day off, he had planned on going in to work for a couple hours until Jace had made him reschedule his day. Stuck babysitting, he wondered if another kid from Danny's Haven needed his help now.

He wasn't sure if he could handle two tripping teens at the same time.

Thinking he never should've been so open about giving the kids his home address and phone number, he glanced into the peephole only to freeze with shock.

CHAPTER NINETEEN

Ansley and Brooklyn stood in the hallway just outside his apartment door.

Ward hadn't seen them for three nights, not since the day they'd all played hooky and gone ice skating. He and Brooklyn had made plans to meet again Monday evening after she got out of school. But he didn't think he'd see or hear from her in between.

Looking at them both now, his heart swelled with a crazy kind of joy. He glanced down at his clothes and groaned. Jace had gotten him out of bed this morning when he'd knocked on Ward's door at barely six a.m. He'd thrown on the first ratted pair of jeans and holey shirt he could find.

Wondering if he had enough time to dash to his room and put on something a little more respectable, he cringed when he saw Ansley shift from leg to leg as if she wanted to escape. Not about to let either of them slip away, he combed down his hair with his hand as he unlocked the door.

"Hey," he said, trying to sound chipper and not at all nervous when he smiled. "This is a surprise. What's going on?"

Ansley looked even more like a flight risk as she met his gaze. She opened her mouth as if she was going to say goodbye when Brooklyn spoke over her.

Lifting a plate in her hands, she said, "We made you cookies." When her mother elbowed her, she cleared her throat and revised, "Okay, so I made you cookies and begged mom to let me bring them over."

Wincing, Ansley added, "I hope we're not interrupting anything. We can leave if you're busy."

"I'm not busy." He opened the door wider. "Come on in."

Brooklyn immediately bounded through the doorway while Ansley hesitated. When Ward lifted an eyebrow, she flushed before murmuring, "Thank you," and stepped past him.

He grew a little carried away inhaling her scent and totally forgot he already had company until he turned around and found both ladies unmoving and gaping at the passed out Jace on his couch.

Crap. He'd forgotten about the boy.

Motioning vaguely, he gave a nervous

laugh. "I'm just babysitting. He's going through some nasty withdrawals and needed a place to crash for a while."

"That's Jace," Brooklyn finally said, cocking her head as she studied him.

Ward narrowed his eyes as he watched her expression. Mostly, she just looked concerned. But he swore he could detect a bit of interest in her gaze as well. He'd definitely have to keep a close eye on those two. If they were anything like him and Ansley at their age, they'd need it.

Shoving his hands into his pockets, he glanced at Ansley as she grasped Brooklyn's arm and met Ward's gaze. "I'm so sorry. We didn't mean to interrupt. We should probably go and let him get his sleep."

He wondered why she was so hesitant about seeing him today. She couldn't seem to hold his stare. As soon as they made eye contact, her brown eyes darted away. She kept wringing her hands too.

"Don't go," he said. "He's fine. He's already been sleeping —" Jace coughed and shifted on the sofa as he stirred. "There." Ward pointed. "He's getting up already."

"Ward?" Jace rasped, his eyes still closed.

"Right here, kiddo." Ward moved to him and crouched by the couch to feel Jace's forehead. Though he was clammy and sweating again, he didn't have a fever. "How you feeling?"

"Like big bird just chewed me up into little pieces and then hacked me up again. I actually had a dream he did just that."

Dropping his hand, Ward chuckled. "Well, you're still in one piece, so there's a plus."

"Does he have a fever?" Brooklyn asked bending down next Ward to feel Jace's forehead as well.

The boy's eyes flashed open. When he blinked at Brooklyn a few times, he bolted upright, clearly alarmed. "You're . . ." His wild gaze darted to Ward, "here."

"My mom and I just stopped by to bring my dad some cookies. Do you want some?"

She lifted the plate to show them off.

Jace stared at them a few seconds before he nodded dumbly. "Okay. Yeah, I could . . ." But his words trailed off as a green tinge suffused his cheeks. Grabbing his stomach, he vaulted off the couch, and mumbled, "Excuse me," as he rushed toward the hallway and disappeared into the bathroom. A split second later, the distinct sound of retching echoed back to them.

Brooklyn glanced down at her plastic-wrapped plate of cookies in horror. "I didn't think they looked that bad."

Ward cracked a grin. "I doubt it was your

cookies. He's been doing this all day. It's all part of the process."

"Well, is he okay?" Ansley asked, her brow knitted with concern. "Should we call a doctor?"

"Na. He'll be —" Ward didn't bother to finish the sentence as Ansley wasn't listening. She'd already followed the sounds Jace was making down the hall to the bathroom.

Ward glanced at Brooklyn, who still looked a little hurt her cookies had made someone empty their stomach. "Trust me, I'll have half that plate polished off by the end of the day. But for now, do you want to sit them on the table for me? Kitchen's right through that doorway."

When she nodded and turned in the direction he was pointing, Ward made his own way to the bathroom. Ansley sat on the floor beside Jace and stroked his back as he choked on air, his stomach lurching with empty spasms.

Looking up at him with worried eyes, she bit her lip, right at the corner. "Nothing's coming out. They're only dry heaves."

Ward leaned against the doorframe, unable to take his eyes off her. She looked so beautiful in all her worried glory. "I'm not surprised. As much stuff that came out of him earlier, I doubt there's anything left in his stomach."

She didn't look pleased by that revelation. "When was the last time he ate?"

With a shrug, Ward told the truth. "I have no idea. He showed up at six this morning and has declined food every time I asked."

"Well, he needs food," she stated decisively. "Brooklyn, go fix him a snack, would you? Something light on his stomach but nutritious enough to sustain him."

Ward glanced askance to realize his daughter had silently appeared at his side. He'd been so entranced in watching Ansley care for the sick teen, he hadn't even noticed.

Brooklyn nodded at her mother's command and once again disappeared.

Jace finally stopped dry heaving only to close his eyes and rest his cheek on the toilet seat.

Studying his face, Ansley ran her fingers over his hair before glancing up at Ward. "Was it like this when you quit, too?"

Ward shook his head. "Na. I had it a lot worse. The kid here hasn't even had one hallucination yet. He's got it lucky."

Jace stirred long enough to mumble, "Braggart," before he wilted back onto the toilet.

Licking her lips, Ansley shook her head sadly. "I can't even imagine."

"Yeah, well . . ." Ward sighed. "That's what we get for destroying our bodies like we did."

"Personally, I don't think anyone deserves this kind of misery." Getting to her feet, Ansley brushed off her knees before gently grasping Jace's shoulders. "Come on, Jace. Let's get you to the kitchen and see what kind of snack Brooklyn is making you."

"Brooklyn?" Jace sounded dazed as he lifted his face. With a nod, he followed her instruction and pushed his way upright.

Still fascinated by Ansley's motherly way with him, Ward stepped out the doorway to let them by as they started for the kitchen. Then he trailed along behind because there was nowhere else he'd rather be but where she was.

Brooklyn already had a pan heating on the stove and was placing cheese slices on a piece of buttered bread when they entered the kitchen.

"Grilled cheese sandwiches. What a good idea, sweetheart," Ansley praised as she led Jace to a chair and sat him down.

When he hunched his shoulder over his body and began to shiver, she turned to Ward. "Could you fetch the blanket from the couch, please? He looks chilled."

Eager to please her, Ward hurried into the

living room. Still disbelieving that this was really happening — Ansley was in his house, with their daughter — and they were helping him care — or actually taking over the care of — one of his teens. It seemed too surreal to believe.

But when he returned to the kitchen, both ladies were still fussing over Jace. Brooklyn offered him a tall glass of milk while Ansley took over at the stove, setting the bread in the heated pan as she advised Jace to drink everything.

Ward watched them from the doorway. Jace glanced between both Ansley and Brooklyn in utter wonder. This was probably the most anyone had ever tended to him. And he bet the kid's crush on his daughter had just skyrocketed, too. It hadn't taken Ward all that long to tumble hard for Ansley. He didn't doubt a boy with his own background would waste much time falling for her daughter, who possessed an amazing soul just like hers.

It all filled him with a nostalgic ache. He wished he could be Jace right now, so both Ansley and Brooklyn could fuss over him. Heck, he'd even take on the kid's withdrawal symptoms to catch this kind of attention. But he doubted Jace would trade him places for anything in the world just now.

Noticing him hesitated in the doorway, Ansley set down the spatula she was using to flip the grilled cheese sandwich. "Oh thanks."

As she approached him, he sucked in a quiet breath, uncertain what to do. What he wanted to do was draw her into his arms and hold her close and never let go, then thank her for being here and doing what she was doing. In his mind, he'd elevated her over the years, making her into this perfect woman. Didn't matter if she'd sent him to jail or not; he'd deserved that and it in no way detracted from his awed perception of her.

What was so incredible was that she was even better than what he'd made her out to be, because now she wasn't the perfect pedestal image of womanhood to him. She was real with flaws — she still grew irritated when it took someone too long to count change, had a problem making up her mind, and let too many other people influence her decisions, plus she'd never even had a happy place until he made her get one — but it was those flaws that made her better, approachable. Touchable.

But he still shouldn't touch her. Ward knew he'd never deserve a woman as grand as Ansley Marlow.

He pulled in his stomach muscles as she came even closer. Dear God, was she going to touch him? He ached for the barest contact from her, his skin was already prickling in preparation.

But instead of landing on him, her fingers wrapped around the throw blanket he'd completely forgotten he still held.

As she tugged it out of his grip, he was tempted to tighten his hold and keep her this close for just a breath longer. He could flicker out a teasing little smile and make her say "please" before releasing his possession of the blanket.

She turned away all too soon and returned to Jace so she could wrap the cover around his shoulders. Still, her gorgeous brown eyes slid his way as she did so, and he languished in the fact that she couldn't seem to look away from him.

Chest full of his craving for her, he smiled and was fulfilled when she smiled back. "Better?" she asked, finally turning her attention to Jace as she patted his shoulder.

Though he continued to shiver, the boy nodded. "Uh, yeah." Flushing, he cleared his throat and plastered his gaze on the tabletop. "Thanks."

"Brooklyn, see if you can find a can of tomato soup. That would go great with his sandwich."

"Oh. Here." Ward stumbled into the kitchen, feeling like a moron with two left feet in his haste to help. "Canned foods are up here." He led his daughter to the correct cupboard and opened the door. He focused his attention on her because — though it still amazed him he had a half-grown daughter — his body didn't surge with an overdose of awareness around her. It just filled him with a warm love that made him want to sling an arm around her shoulder and smell her hair. His daughter's hair. Wow, he loved saying that.

His daughter.

As he and his daughter prepared the soup together — simply opening the can, dumping the contents into a bowl, stirring in a little milk and heating it in the microwave — Ansley finished the grilled sandwich.

"What's this?" Jace asked from where he shook in his chair as he set his empty glass of milk on the table. Reaching for the plate of cookies, he slid it aside to reveal an album of some kind underneath.

Ward frowned at it since he knew it wasn't his. "I don't —"

"Oh, I brought that," Brooklyn said and bit her lip as she turned to Ward. "It's . . . well, it's my baby album that Mom put together. I thought . . . I thought maybe you'd like to see some pictures of me through the years."

"Really?" Ward said, feeling honored. Tightness swelled in his throat. As much as he wanted to see every picture, he already knew it would hurt, because he'd get to actually see how much of her life he'd missed. But no way was he not looking. He pressed a fist to his mouth and cleared his throat. "Yeah. Yes, I'd love that. Very much."

He stepped to the table where Jace had already pulled open the front cover. Ward could only gape at the small newborn infant he saw on the first page, cradled in the arms of a fifteen-year-old Ansley lying in a hospital bed. Despite how tired and worn she appeared, she grinned with pride.

Blinking away tears, Ward wiped a hand over his mouth as Jace turned the page. Jace leaned forward and unknowingly crowded Ward to the side as he read the captions Ansley had handwritten next to each photo.

Ansley interrupted them when she set the grilled cheese on a plate in front of Jace.

Snagging up the sandwich like the starving teen he was, Jace bit off a mouthful and glanced up at her. "You made this book?" he asked as he chewed. "This is really awesome."

"It was nothing." She blushed and shifted her arms as if she didn't know what to do with them. "Every mom does it."

Jace snorted. "Not my mom." He flipped a page as he tore off another hearty bite with his teeth. "I had a foster parent take a few pictures of me when I was little, but when I went back to my real mom, she went on a rant when she got high one night and ended up tearing them all to shreds."

Brooklyn gasped as she pulled out a chair and sat next to him. "No way. Why would she do that?"

With a shrug, Jace turned the page. "I don't know. That's just the way she is."

Ansley looked at Ward. "Did your mom make you a baby album?"

"Uh." He felt singled out as he shifted uncomfortably and scratched at the back of his neck. "Kind of."

She crinkled her nose. "What does kind of mean?"

"She began one, I think. I found out about it when my first half-sister was born, and my mom started putting together an album for her. I remember watching her work so diligently and asked if she'd made one like that for me, too. She said something about how there were too many pictures of my dad in it, so she threw it away."

Ansley's mouth dropped open. "Your mother threw out all your baby pictures?"

In a hushed voice, Brooklyn croaked, "That's awful."

Ward exchanged a knowing glance with Jace. Feeling a kinship, he realized that after surviving through the childhoods they'd each had, they both understood how truly important keeping up a baby album was.

Brooklyn seemed to realize it too. She reached out almost hesitantly and touched one of her own pictures through its thin film covering. "This really is nice, Mom." She smiled at Ansley. "Thank you."

Again, Ansley didn't seem to know what to do with all the flattery. Rolling her eyes at her daughter, she snagged the empty glass Jace had set down and hurried to the sink where she began to rinse and clean it.

Studying the tense set of her shoulders, Ward frowned. He had praised her a lot when they'd been kids — always telling her how pretty, and smart, and sweet he thought she was — and she hadn't had any problems receiving compliments then.

Hands balling into fists, he wondered what kind of guilt job her parents had done to her since she'd conceived Brooklyn. They'd torn down a part of her soul, and he just wanted to build it back up.

Leaving the kids at the table still skimming through Brooklyn's baby album, he strolled toward the sink.

"You're not doing my dishes, are you?" he asked in a low, teasing voice.

Ansley jumped and whirled around. "Oh, I just —" She glanced down at the clean, wet cup in her hands and gave a guilty laugh. "Yes, I guess I am."

"Well, don't." Gently, he slid the glass and drying towel from her hands. "This isn't your job."

With her hands free, she folded them at her waist and sent him a tense smile. "I just wanted to help."

He laughed. "I don't think you have any idea how much you already have." Lowering his voice, he stepped closer and nodded his head Jace's way. "Trust me, you helped. You've done more for him in the past five minutes than his own mother has in seventeen years. I'd watch out if I were you, he might hide out in your trunk when you leave so he can follow you home and adopt you."

The tops of Ansley's cheeks brightened with color. "Oh, I'm sure I didn't do all that much."

Stone, cold sober, Ward met her gaze. "Yes, you did."

Blush dying a quick death, Ansley sent

Jace a concerned look as her brow crinkled with worry. Ward could actually read her thoughts. She just might want to adopt Jace too and bring him home with her. "But he's such a nice boy," she said softly. "How could a mother do that?"

Ward looked down at his hands. "Probably the same way a father could abandon his daughter for sixteen years."

Flashing him an irritated glower, Ansley hissed, "That's completely different. You wanted Brooklyn to have the best chance possible. Self-sacrifice out of love is nothing like . . . like neglect."

She spun away to wrap her hands around the lip of the sink and stare out his kitchen window. Ward leaned a hip against the counter beside her.

"I'm just glad Brooklyn had you all these years."

Instead of responding to that, she said in a dazed voice, "You have a hummingbird feeder."

He turned and glanced out the window to see the empty feeder he'd left hanging outside from the windowsill. He usually took it down for the winter by now. He hadn't seen any birds at it for a couple of months. They've probably already migrated south.

Now, as he stared at the hanging glass tube with the red and yellow adornments, he wished he'd remembered.

Too much seemed to be revealed in this one bird feeder.

He'd already told Ansley how much hummingbirds reminded him of her. Now she would know how much he'd drawn the birds to him so he could keep as many memories of her alive in him as he could. She'd know how much he never stopped thinking of her, never stopped loving her.

He couldn't speak as she turned slowly to look at him. His mouth opened but no words came. Looking into her knowing brown eyes, he could tell she knew everything. His heart, his mind, his soul.

Feeling like an open book, he stared back as she read him.

When a smile lit her lips, he released all the air he'd been holding in his lung with a rush.

"Hey, what're you two doing over there?" Brooklyn called, making both her parents give a guilty start and spin her way.

Ward was the first to collect his scattered wits. "I'm just waiting for Jace there to stop hogging your baby album so I can finally look at it," he said with a forced ornery grin full of mischievous teasing.

"Hey, man. Wait your turn. I'm not done yet." The kid arched him a defiant look and purposely turned another page.

Ward sent Ansley a sigh that said, see-what-I-have-to-put-up-with and they shared a grin. Though the intensity of the moment before had broken, he still liked the friendly camaraderie he could share with her too. He just hoped he didn't do anything to mess it up this time around.

CHAPTER TWENTY

"Man, you got it bad."

Ward turned from his front door and released the knob he'd just used to close it. After seeing his daughter and her mother off, he already felt like a huge hole had formed inside him.

"What?" he asked Jace with raised eyebrows.

The boy snickered. "You have the major hots for your baby's mama."

"Whatever." Ward rolled his eyes and strode across the living room to head to the kitchen as if he needed to clean it up, even though Ansley had completely ignored his warnings and done all the dishes anyway. He'd only let her because he'd insisted on drying.

Not about to give up on their conversation, a surprisingly healthy-looking Jace followed him. "Oh, I saw the way you looked when she touched your arm as she said goodbye. She just touched your arm, man, and I swear little hearts started circling your head."

Ward laughed, completely embarrassed now, because the kid was right. Ansley's mere touch got him riled up until he wanted to burst. "Shut up."

"What? It was cute. You should ask her out."

Skidding to a halt in the opening of the kitchen, Ward veered around. "Ask her out? I can't ask her out." Was the kid insane?

With the blanket Ansley had wrapped around his shoulder still firmly in place, Jace held the front together and shrugged. "Why not?"

Ward went blank. Why not? He tried to think up all the obvious reasons but couldn't drum up a single one. There was Brooklyn to consider, of course. He didn't want to do anything to hurt her. But if he and Ansley reconnected, then he'd only get to see more of his daughter. And if they, by chance, married someday, he could be a full-time dad and —

Reality crashed through him. What was he thinking? Marry Ansley? She should never have to settle for an ex-addict. She should have a . . . another doctor. Not one that called her names and made her feel bad about herself, but she should get a rich, successful man that could adorn her with anything her heart desired.

"And she wants you right back," Jace drawled in a taunting voice. "I can't tell which one of you has it worse."

His resolve wavered. Casting the teen a sideways glance, he said, "You think?" Ansley really wanted him? He wanted her to have everything she wanted. But if she wanted him —

Could he even allow himself to hope it was true?

"And I gotta tell you," Jace ranted on. "You're sickeningly sappy when you're in love. Seriously, man. Gag me. You didn't even touch her and I wanted to warn you about PDA."

Ward laughed. "I was not that bad."

"Were too."

Refraining from entering a taunting argument with the kid, Ward grinned and leaned against the arched opening of his kitchen with a wistful sigh. "You really don't think it would be inappropriate if I asked her out?"

Tucking the blanket closer around him, Jace curled up on the couch, still looking a little pale. "Why would it be?"

Ward shrugged. "I don't know. But what

about Brooklyn? Do you think it would upset her if —"

"Na. She'd love it. She told me she couldn't wait until you asked her mom out already."

Cocking a suspicious eyebrow, Ward demanded, "When did she tell you this?"

Jace yawned and closed his eyes as he rested his cheek on the back of the couch. "When you and Ansley were whispering and flirting while you did dishes together."

They really had been kind of flirting, hadn't they? He hadn't even realized. Realizing it now, he tensed, wishing he could've had just a little more time with her . . . out of view of a couple snoopy teens.

He pushed away from the doorway. "I'm going to ask her out," he said with sudden resolve.

"Good." Jace's voice slurred as sleep began to claim him. "Do it."

"Right now."

"About time."

Ward paused as he studied Jace. What if the boy had another relapse while he was gone? Hesitating, he shifted, uncertain. "Would you be okay here if I stepped out for a few minutes?"

But Jace didn't answer. He was already fast asleep.

■ ■ ■ ■

Ansley had only been home five minutes when her cell phone rang. She and Brooklyn had stayed at Ward's until later than her usual bedtime. Brooklyn had stumbled off to her own room as soon as they'd made it home, mumbling a half-hearted goodnight. But Ansley didn't feel exhausted in the least.

Jazzed and antsy, not sure what to do with the excess energy racing through her, she answered the phone without checking the ID.

"Hey," Ward's voice filled her ear, making her body lurch with even more vivacity. Great. Now she'd never get to sleep tonight. "Where's Brooklyn?" he asked, his voice curious yet cautious.

"She's already gone to bed." Ansley frowned, confused. "Did you need to talk to her?" He already had Brooklyn's cell phone number; why hadn't he called it directly?

Ward hesitated. "No. Actually, I was wondering if I could talk to you a few minutes . . . alone."

Dread immediately filled her. This did not sound good. Did he want to fight for custody of Brooklyn after all?

"Um . . ." She bit her lip. "Sure. Okay.

What's up?" *Please don't say something bad, please don't say something bad.* She'd had such a lovely evening. She, and Brooklyn, and Ward, and even Jace meshed together perfectly, teasing, joking, laughing. They'd felt like a complete family. She'd wanted it to last forever. The only thing that would've made it better was if she could've snuck in a little alone time with Ward.

"Great. My truck's outside in your driveway if you want to meet me out here."

Ansley spun toward the nearest window that faced her driveway. "You're here? Right now?"

Holy cow, he was. She could see the red glow of his parking lights as his truck sat behind her car.

He chuckled, and the sound captured her heart. "Yes. Is that okay? We could either sit out here and talk or drive somewhere. Your choice."

A reckless kind of euphoria flooded her senses. "Let's drive somewhere," she answered. "I'll be right out."

She hung up without saying goodbye. Instead of racing to the door, she rushed to her room. Checking out her reflection in her mirror, she mussed her hair, giving it a little life, readjusted her bra to perk the girls up some, and bit her lips to make them a little redder. If she had enough time, she'd shower and change outfits and reapply her makeup. But there was no time.

Ward was here!

And they were going to drive off some-where together. Just the two of them. Thrilled she was finally going to get that alone time with him she'd been craving, she hurried out the door, barely remembering to grab a coat and tuck it under her arm as she went. She was kind of glad she didn't put it on. It was so cold outside she had a great excuse to run to his truck without looking too eager.

"Hi," she said, out of breath, as she opened the passenger side door and hopped inside. A vapor fog from her lips followed her inside, and she immediately pressed her chilled hands to the heater on his dash.

"There was no hurry. You could've paused to put your coat on, you know." He sounded amused as he watched her warm her fingers.

"Oh. Well, a little running is good for the lungs."

He watched her, a strange gleam lighting his eyes as if he knew better. Checking her hands, she pressed them to her cheeks to see if they were still cold. But her cheeks were so frozen, she couldn't tell.

Ward shook his head, looking a little too

entertained. "Ready?"

When she nodded, he put the truck into reverse and pulled them out of her driveway. He started down the street away from her house, and she remembered the dread she'd felt about his wanting to speak to her alone.

"Was there anywhere you wanted to go?" he asked as if this whole outing had been her idea, when okay, maybe it had been. Maybe she'd wished for some alone time with him so hard it had actually come true.

She shrugged. "Anywhere is fine." As long as it was with him. After clearing her throat, she added, "So . . . uh, what did you want to talk about? Custody of Brooklyn?"

He winced and kept his eyes on the road. "Not exactly."

Oh, God. He did want custody, didn't he? How much: full or partial? Did he plan on making a fuss and fighting dirty for her?

"What does not exactly mean?" she had to know.

Ward pulled to a curb and she realized he'd stopped at the park closest to her house. At this time of night, it was deserted. But the streetlights sprayed down on the swing set jumble gym perfectly.

"Do you want to get out and walk around?" he asked quietly.

She pulled her coat closer to her chest.

"It's warmer in here. What exactly did you want to talk about?"

His jaw bunched as if he was gritting his teeth, then he shifted on the seat as he turned to face her. His eyes looked extra blue, which was strange since she could barely see him in the darkened interior of his cab.

Taking a quick breath, he answered, "I wanted to talk about . . . us."

Ansley blinked, not soaking in his words. It took her brain a second to process. Then she shook her head, confused and commanding herself not to be hopeful. "What about us?"

He opened his mouth, paused, then looked down at his hands. "What I'm about to suggest is the craziest, insane thing ever. You'd be a fool to agree but I'm going to ask it anyway."

Ansley gave a hesitant bob of her head. "Okay. Go ahead." Her mind raced, and her heart wasn't too far behind. He wasn't actually going to ask . . . was he?

Oh God, she hoped so.

He blew out a long breath. "I know I don't have much. I'm not a wealthy surgeon and have no ties to Harvard medical school. My past is, well . . . awful, which you already know all about. And my future doesn't hold

282

a lot of financial security. But I —"

"Yes!" she cried out, leaping across the bench seat to kiss him.

He caught her halfway and met her lips with a bone-jarring crash. She felt the impact all the way to the soles of her feet. They laughed and pressed noses together before he tipped his chin to the side and slid his mouth across hers with a lot more finesse but the same punch of awareness as their first attempt.

She cupped his head, delighting in the feel of his dark hair under her fingers. He barely brushed his fingers over the tendons of her neck, stroking her throat until she went liquid limp against him, molding to his will.

The kiss lingered and lasted, rolling into another and yet another. When he pulled back to rest his cheek against hers, his breath was unsteady.

"I'm sorry to put the brakes on this because I don't want to stop kissing you, like ever. But . . . just to be clear, what exactly are you saying yes to?"

"I . . ." Eyes flaring wide, Ansley pulled back in horror, realizing, "I guess I don't know."

Now she felt like a colossal idiot. Her stupid hopes and dreams had gotten the best of her and now she was assuming he was asking something there was no way he'd really be asking.

"What . . . what were you asking me?" she said in a hesitant voice.

He shook his head. "No way. You first."

She grinned and rolled her eyes. "No, no, no. Finish your question? I swear, I'll listen to the whole thing first this time."

The shaking of his head grew more insistent. But at least he grinned at her, looking pleased. That was a good sign. "No. You tell me what you were approving first. Because I plan to revise what I was going to say to fit whatever you thought I meant."

Her smile fell flat. Closing her eyes, she buried her face into her hands. "I am such a fool. You weren't asking me to marry you. Were you?"

"Marry you?" he breathed out the word, sounding startled to the core, which told her, no, he definitely hadn't been proposing.

She couldn't take the mortification. They were only five blocks from home. She should escape and run that way right now. No way could she stay in his truck with him a second longer.

But when she reached for the door handle, it was his turn to leap across the seat.

"Whoa! Wait, just wait. Where're you going?"

She couldn't look at him after what she'd just done, so she continued to face the passenger side door. "I can walk home from here," she managed to choke out in a hoarse voice.

"No, you most certainly cannot. Ansley, look at me."

The gentleness of his hands on her shoulders made her cringe before she slowly came around.

"The only reason I hadn't planned on proposing tonight was because I thought it was way too soon. I thought we needed more time to get to know the present-day Ansley and Ward."

Wincing she bobbed her head in immediate agreement. "You're right. It's way too soon. We should —"

He set a finger over her mouth, silencing her. With an amused grin, he lifted an eyebrow and asked, "May I finish?"

Remaining mute, she nodded.

Chuckling softly, he gazed over her face and took his finger away from her mouth to run his touch over her hair. "I do want to marry you. Tomorrow, if you'd have me. But I was going to try to be a gentleman and slowly work my way up to it and maybe ask you out first. Start with a single date. I know we have . . . something. And I wanted to explore it because what I feel for you now is even stronger than what I felt seventeen years ago. But I didn't want to rush you. What I mean is . . ." With a groan, he closed his eyes and ran his hands down his face. "Oh, God. I'm so messing this up."

She grinned. "No, you're not."

He dropped his fingers to his sides and opened his eyes. "I'm not?"

Beaming, she shook her head. "Not at all."

Relief showed on his face as Ward slid closer to her, only to jerk to an immediate stop, uncertainty clouding his features. "Does that mean . . ."

She bit the corner of her bottom lip. "I love you more now than I did seventeen years ago too, Ward. And seventeen years ago, you were everything to me."

"Holy crap, you just said you love me," he breathed out in utter awe. "This can't be happening."

"I'm sorry," she started, clenching her teeth because she was pushing everything when really, she didn't want to push at all. "I wasn't going to say anything. I didn't want you to feel pressured but —"

"I love you, too," he said just before pressing his mouth against hers.

She laughed because life was too beautiful at the moment not to. Drinking from her lips, Ward groaned deep in his throat and spoke against her mouth. "This is when someone inevitably knocks on the door to interrupt us."

She opened her mouth to gainsay him. But he held up a finger. "It's happens every time. Just wait for it." He even glanced over his shoulder at the driver's side of his truck door.

Rolling her eyes, she grasped his face and urged him around. "Not this time."

He laughed as she kissed him, the vibrations causing a warm stir in her belly.

And his cell phone rang from his pocket.

"I don't hear anything. Do you hear anything?" he asked and kissed her even more deeply than before.

The phone continued to ring.

Ansley pulled back. "What if it's Brooklyn? I didn't tell her where I was going and I think I left my phone at the house."

Ward closed his eyes and panted a moment before lifting up in his seat to pull his phone from his pocket. He made a face and grumbled under his breath.

"It's Caren. Probably about work. I should take this."

CHAPTER TWENTY-ONE

"I need you to come into Danny's Haven," Care said as soon as Ward answered the phone.

And here, he felt he needed to dive across the seat of his truck and continue making out with the lovely lady beside him.

Ansley wanted to marry him.

He still couldn't wrap his brain around that. She wanted to marry him, spend the rest of her life with him and be his wife. And she'd said yes to him before he could even ask. With that doctor fellow, it had taken her time to think before she could turn him down. An immediate yes — which was a heck of a lot bigger decision than a no — was a very good, very promising sign.

He felt drugged as he'd never felt drugged before, high on the euphoria of life, as he met her soft, brown-eyed gaze and said into the phone, "Right now? This late?"

"Yes, right now." Care hissed into his ear.

"This late."

She sounded off balance. Care was never out of sorts. He frowned and focused a little more on the call. "What's going on? Everything okay?"

"No, everything is not okay. That's why I need you to come in. Right now."

"Okay. Give me a couple minutes. I'll be right there."

As he disconnected, he met Ansley's gaze again. She bit her lip, looking adorable and concerned all in the same glance. "Duty calls, huh?"

He shook his head and put the truck into drive. "Apparently. I'm sorry, An—"

"Don't be. I'm actually very proud of you. You've come so far from the boy you used to be, Ward. Now you get late night calls because your work finds you irreplaceable. That's . . . that's wonderful."

He laughed. "Yeah, and you may be the only wife on the planet that feels that way when her husband is called away."

Ansley sucked in a breath. "Wife?" she strangled out the word.

Realizing what he'd just called her, Ward didn't answer as he pulled into her driveway and parked. Finally, he turned to her, and reached out to pull her close. Their faces nearly touching, he said, "You really don't think I'm going to let you take back that 'yes' you said, do you?"

She bit the corner of her lip. "But I didn't know what I was saying yes to."

Searching her eyes, he touched her cheek. "Well, you do now. I want to marry you. Someday. It doesn't have to be today, or tomorrow. We can date as long as you like, get to know each other, reconnect. I don't care. I just want to be with you."

She closed her eyes and leaned forward to rest her forehead against his chin. "That's what I want, too," she confessed on a whisper.

Sliding his fingers down along her jaw until he cupped her cheek, he lifted her face. "Then, that's what you'll get. We'll work out the details along the way."

When he pressed his mouth to hers, she wrapped her arms around his neck and clung to him. Two minutes later, she pulled away with a miserable groan. "Okay, I'm beginning to see why wives don't like their husbands to be called away. But you have troubled teens to save, so . . . I guess I'll let you go."

"I'll call you tomorrow?" he asked, kissing her cheek, then her jaw. The side of her neck. Finally, she shifted far enough away he couldn't kiss anything else.

"You better." She sent him a dazzling smile that made him want to leap at her again and tug her back into his arms. Where she belonged. But she opened her door and slid out.

"Wait. I'll walk you to your door."

He began to reach for his door handle, but she called, "Nope. Too dangerous. I might not let you leave if you do." Then shutting him inside the truck alone, she dashed to her back porch.

Shaking his head, Ward stayed in her driveway until she'd disappeared inside and turned on her kitchen light. With a regretful sigh, he reversed his truck back onto the street.

Danny's Haven looked quiet and commotion-free when Ward walked through the front doors. Usually, someone was stirring. Most of the teens who sought them for help were night owls and someone or another was always awake, watching a movie or playing in the game room. But the only girl he saw tonight was Tara, who lay curled on one of the large couches sleeping peacefully.

Not spotting Care around, he meandered to her office, twirling his key ring around his finger and humming under his breath.

When he realized he was singing the tune of the wedding march, he grinned.

Ansley was going to be his wife someday. It didn't seem real.

Care's office door was shut, so he tapped on it quietly.

"Come in," his mentor called.

Ward turned the handle and entered. When he saw the well-dressed man seated in front of her desk, he gave the guy in the dark trench coat, designer khaki slacks, hushpuppy loafers, and gold Rolex a respectful nod in acknowledgement before approaching Care's desk. In return, the man merely stared at him with an assessing, yet condescending glare.

"What's going on?" he asked.

Care's lips pressed tight together as she motioned to the second chair beside the stranger. "Take a seat, Ward."

Wondering if she'd called him in for another bogus intervention, he sat, cast the rude guy a curious glance, and turned back to his boss, waiting for her to begin.

She nodded at Trench Coat and said, "I believe you know Dr. Preston Jackson."

He began to shake his head, since he'd never seen this guy before in his life. But a second later, his name sank in and he froze. Slowly, he turned to inspect the man who'd called Ansley atrocious names.

"No," he murmured in a steely soft voice. "We haven't met."

Care pursed her eyebrows as if doubting him. "Really? Well, he's here to claim you stole prescription drugs from his fiancée's medicine cabinet."

"Huh?" Ward's mouth fell open as he gaped as his mentor.

She nodded, telling him it was true. Eyes narrowing, she glared at Ward as if upset with him for putting her through this situation. "And he's oh-so graciously agreed to keep quiet about it if I terminate your employment at Danny's Haven."

Dr. Jackson leaned toward them, finally added his two cents. "I wouldn't feel right knowing a confirmed and active drug user was working with teens to prevent their own drug activities."

He was able to sound so concerned — it was enough to make Ward want to stick his finger in his mouth and pretend to puke.

Instead, Ward shook his head and barked out a full belly laugh. "This is ridiculous." He pushed to his way to his feet, already ready to leave. "You know he's lying," he told his boss who remained seated behind her desk with her hands firmly clasped on top. "Why did you even bother me for this?"

Turning away he started for the door, too angry to even see straight.

But Care's voice stopped him. "Ward, I don't want this kind of light shown on Danny's Haven."

After stopping in his tracks, he slowly turned around. She couldn't be serious. But the expression on her face was pretty, freaking stoic.

He swallowed, feeling suddenly unsure about his job.

As if she could read his fears, her face softened. "You know the slightest hint of gossip, no matter how untrue it is can discredit our entire organization. Everything we've worked years to accomplish . . . down the drains in a snap of the fingers."

Ward could only stare at her and shake his head. "So you're just going to give into his blackmail? This is insane. You know I'm clean."

"I'm thinking about the center here."

"And what about your most dedicated employee?" His yelled, poking a finger into the center of his chest. "I have put my heart and soul into Danny's Haven. You can't deny that. I have worked overtime more times than I haven't. I have wept, and laughed, and bled to help every single kid out there. I have stood up in front of thousands — thousands — of people and told them about the most humiliating parts of my life . . . because you asked me to. I did that for you. I would give my life for you."

She sniffed and lowered her face. "I'm sorry."

And yet, she was still willing to fire him at the drop of a hat. He felt strangely empty.

Balling his hands, he swung toward Jackson. The pathetic doctor actually flinched back and lifted his hands as if to protect himself. Ward shook his head. What a moron.

"If you want to make yourself look like a jealous fool, go ahead and cry wolf." Ward shrugged as if he didn't care. Which he didn't. He knew he was safe. "I took a drug test very recently and I'll go to the hospital right now and taken another. They won't find one illegal substance in my system."

Jackson shrugged too, though his eyes cooled with distaste. "Maybe you're not taking them personally. Maybe you're supplying them to these poor children you're supposed to be rehabilitating."

"Oh, so now I'm a drug dealer, is that it? Classic. You are so full of —"

"Ward!" Care surged to her feet as if she was going to dash around her desk to slap the back of his hand with a ruler.

He sliced her a single glower before turning back to Jackson. "You know what? Ansley told you no. You need to accept that and move on. Attacking me won't help you get her back."

Pinching up his face as if trying to block the fact that Ward had made a direct hit, the manipulating doctor slowly rose to his feet as well. Straightening the lapels of his name brand trench coat, he studied Ward as he would an insect he wanted to squash but didn't want to ruin the soles of his name brand shoes to step on.

"This isn't about getting her back," he said, making it sound as if that had never been his intention. "I care about her and want what's best for her." His gaze skimmed Ward, clearly conveying he didn't think Ward was best for her.

Ward snorted. "Yeah, because nothing says I love you like calling the woman you asked to marry a whore and a trollop."

Flushing, the doctor glanced at Care before clearing his throat. "Well, I've said all I was going to say. You have my ultimatum. He goes or I start talking to the press." With that, he brushed past Ward and strolled to the exit.

As soon as the door clicked shut, Ward

spun toward Caren. "Why are you letting a bully boss you around and dictate what you do?"

She sank back into her chair to cradle her head in her hands. "You know, I had reservations about hiring an ex user into my clinic, but you proved yourself worthy." Until now, her hard cold look added as she lifted her face. "But I have to look at the big picture here."

He shook his head. "I thought you at least believed in me."

When she didn't answer, his soul ripped away from his chest. Drenched in pain, he turned away.

"Ward . . ."

He stopped but didn't turn back.

She growled out a sound of frustration. "This is all that woman's fault. I knew from the moment she came back into your life, she'd manage to rip you away from us."

Ward's jaw tightened, shocked she would even mention Ansley, much less blame anything on her. Spinning back, he snapped, "No! She has nothing to with this. You're the one pushing me out the door."

"And you've already been gone for weeks, since the day you met your daughter. Your attention hasn't been here, at Danny's Haven. It's been with them."

Sputtering an incredulous laugh, he stared at the woman he'd worshipped for the past seven years. It hurt to see her turn away from him. It hurt to know she'd never returned any of his affections.

But she was right. Nothing meant as much to him as Ansley and Brooklyn did. Not even Danny's Haven. With a nod, he said, "Well, thank you for pointing out to me what's truly important in my life. I'll start cleaning out my office now."

This time, when he walked from her room, she didn't call after him.

CHAPTER TWENTY-TWO

Jace was still asleep when Ward made it home from the center. He carried a box of his belongings from his office with him, clutching it to his chest. As the door shut at his back, he leaned against it to watch the boy on his couch.

This still didn't seem real. He was no longer a drug counselor. What was he supposed to do with his life now?

He'd have to find a job as fast as possible, because it wasn't like he had a lot of money sitting around to pay the bills while he was unemployed, except that little nest egg he'd saved for Brooklyn. And no way was he taking her money. She'd need it for —

Wait.

Brooklyn. Ansley.

How was he supposed to tell them he'd been fired, and his reputation as a counselor was now on shaky ground? With the revenge-seeking mad doctor set on his selfish rampage, Ward may never get another job in the same field of employment.

And helping teens was in his blood.

Jumping when Jace mumbled something in his sleep and shifted from his side to his stomach, Ward slid down the door until he was sitting on the floor. He'd never be able to help anyone like Jace again.

Ward sat there for a long time, thinking, planning, and coming up with no easy solution. He couldn't continue anything with Ansley without some kind of respectable employment. No way was he going to let her date — much less marry — a jobless bum.

But after the start he'd had, his life skills were sadly lacking. Outside some back-breaking factory labor or the fast food industry, he wasn't sure he could do much of anything.

The night seeped by as his brain scrambled for some kind of alternative out of his predicament. At some point, he dragged himself back to his feet and stumbled off to his room, but he didn't get much sleep.

Up early, he left while Jace was still out. The boy was still asleep when he returned. So Ward slid into a chair, letting the shopping bag he brought in with him drop by his feet. And he watched his young friend for over an hour until Jace finally stirred.

Hair flat against his face on one side and standing straight up on the other, Jace sat up and stretched with a hearty yawn. Wincing at Ward, he wiped the sleep from his face. He was still a little pale and drawn, but he wasn't trembling or acting as if his nerves were on overdrive. He didn't grab his stomach and race toward the bathroom. He looked as if he'd fared the storm and made it through.

Scowling at him, Jace patted at his hair as he yawned again. "You didn't have to take off work today just to babysit me," Jace said.

Ward's jaw tightened. He couldn't tell the kid he didn't have any work to go to anymore, so he shrugged. "It's Sunday. I wasn't scheduled to go in anyway."

Before Jace could respond, he picked up the plastic bag. "Hey, I went out before you got up this morning. These are for you."

After he tossed the sack toward the couch and it landed in the teen's lap, Jace peeked inside. "Clothes?"

With a shrug, Ward answered, "Yeah. The jeans you're wearing now are looking a little too frayed to be fashionable." And since this was probably the last time he'd see the kid, he wanted to do something as a farewell.

Glancing down at his hands, he tried to breathe around the knot in his throat. He was going to miss Jace the most.

"You didn't have to buy me clothes." The boy sounded a little panicked as if he wasn't sure how to handle an act of kindness.

On the flip side, Ward had never known how to accept gratitude. He stared at his shoes and shrugged. "Well, I was tired of looking at you in the same thing day in and day out. I needed a change of scenery."

Jace snorted as if he was going to spit back another insult, but instead he ducked his head and mumbled, "Well . . . thanks."

Ward nodded. Lifting his face, he stared at Jace hard. "Promise me you'll take care of yourself, okay. Once you get past this round of detoxing, you could be home free in the physical effects department. Your body won't need anything to depend on. You don't have to go back. Ever again."

Jace narrowed his eyes as if trying to figure out Ward's words. Then he shrugged. "I don't plan on going back. Man, you're not buying me clothes to keep from doing drugs, are you?"

Ward chuckled. "No, I just . . . you're one of my favorites, and I wanted you to have something, anything. I wish I could give you a better life all the way around, but all I can afford are a stupid pair of jeans."

Throwing the blanket off him, Jace surged to his feet and loomed over Ward. "Okay, now you're starting to freak me out. What's going on? What's up with all this mushy crap like you're saying goodbye forever or something? Do you want me to leave, is that it? Cause all you have to do is tell me I've overstayed my welcome. I'll go."

"No, I don't want you to leave." Ward winced and rubbed his face. "In fact, if you ever need a place to stay again, I hope I'm the first person you come to. If you need help, I will help you. You know that, right?"

Jace just started at him. "What aren't you telling me?" he demanded in a low, serious voice. "Are you dying or something?"

Ward sighed and closed his eyes. "No. It's . . . nothing. Just . . . go try on your clothes. See if any of them actually fit. I kept the receipt in the bag in case you need, or just want, to exchange anything."

"Ward!" Jace shouted this time. When Ward glanced up, the teen whispered in a trembling, frightened voice, "What's going on?"

Someone knocked — or more like pounded — on his apartment door, relieving him from answering.

Anxious for a distraction, Ward popped to his feet. "Excuse me."

CHAPTER TWENTY-THREE

The two females he saw through his peep-hole made Ward jerk the door open. "Desi? Tara? What're you guys doing here?"

"We're not staying there with that witch." Desi bulldozed past him to enter his apartment but skidded to a stop when she saw Jace. "What the heck are you doing here?" Then she smiled and nodded as if in approval. "So you're supporting the Ward man too, huh? Good."

Lifting her fist for the boy to bump it, she dropped her hand when Jace scowled at her. "What the heck are you talking about? What's going on?"

"Caren fired Ward last night," Tara spoke up. "I was there and heard everything through the door of her office."

Ward's mouth fell open, surprised she'd actually been awake. He'd been avoiding Tara a lot lately since he'd confessed his jail time for rape. With her background, he didn't want her to feel uncomfortable in his presence.

But when she looked up at him, she didn't look uncomfortable in the least. "I can't believe she did that to you. You're the best counselor at Danny's Haven and the only . . . man I've ever felt safe around. What she did to you wasn't fair at all."

"And when Tara called me this morning and told me what happened, I turned in my own resignation," Desi added, slinging her arm around Tara's shoulder. "No one treats you like that and gets away with it."

"Wait!" Jace waved his hands and stepped forward. "What happened? Why would anyone fire Ward?"

Tara and Desi took turns filling him in on what had happened the night before.

"Are you freaking kidding me? There's no way they could prove he fell off the wagon. He just took a drug test like, last week?"

"This is unheard of," Desi railed. "Plain and simple. If that idiot woman was so worried about her precious center's reputation, she never should've pushed you out. I have a mind to contact the papers and come up with my own lie to give her the gossip she was so adamant to avoid."

"No." Ward grabbed her shoulder to calm her down. "You will do no such thing. No matter what happened to me, or any of us, Danny's Haven's motto is still pure and honest with the goal to help troubled teens. You are not jeopardizing that because of a vendetta."

"Well, I wasn't there because of the Danny's Haven motto," Tara said. "I was there because of you. You were the first person to talk to me when I walked through that door, and you were the reason I stayed. I go where you go."

"But I . . ." He floundered. "I have nowhere to go."

Tara just started at him, her heart in her eyes and her trust in him. "Then make us somewhere new to go," she said simply.

Her faith in him rocked him to his core. He opened his mouth to thank her unquestioning support and then tell her her wish wasn't possible to grant when someone else knocked on his door.

"Geez Louise," Jace grumbled. "It's like Grand Central Station around here. How's a guy supposed to detox?"

"That better be Care, begging you to come back." Desi strode to the door before Ward could do so.

Bemused by her take-charge demeanor, he shook his head and watched as she arched up onto her tiptoes to check the peephole. The next visitor must've been someone she wanted to see because she ripped open the door, saying, "It's about time you got here."

Ward peered around her, expecting to see Care. But he was shocked to find a completely different pair of ladies on his doorstep.

The sight of Ansley and Brooklyn made his heart drop into his stomach. He sent his co-worker, or whatever Desi was to him now, a hard look. "You called them over?"

Great. They must already know everything now.

"Of course I didn't." Desi sent him an eye-roll. "I figured you had though." When Ward just looked at her, she scowled. "What? Haven't you told them yet?"

"What's going on?" Brooklyn asked, skipping inside and stopping when she saw Tara and Jace. Blushing, she smiled bashfully at the boy. "Hi again."

Ward ripped a hand through his hair. Too much. This was all just too much.

How was he supposed to explain all this to Ansley? How was he supposed to look her in the eye and tell her he couldn't see her again until he was worthy and had his life back on track?

"Is everything okay?" she asked, her

brown eyes full of concern.

"No," Desi answered for him, grabbing Ansley's arm and tugging her into the apartment. "Everything is one big, stupid mess." And she — with the help of Tara and Jace — proceeded to catch Ansley and Brooklyn up to speed.

Ansley covered her mouth with both hands and turned to Ward, her eyes widened in horror. "This is all my fault," she whispered. "I told him you'd taken that bottle of pills and gotten rid of it because I didn't need his prescription anymore."

"This is not your fault." Ward reached for her, only to drop his hand, telling himself he didn't have to right to touch her now.

"Too bad you flushed all the pills," Brooklyn said. "We could prove you never took them."

Ward frowned. "I didn't flush them."

Ansley looked up, blinking. "But . . . but you said you'd gotten rid of them."

"I didn't flush them," he repeated. "I didn't want them to get back into the water system, so I just threw them in your trash."

"You . . . Oh!" Her face brightened with delight. "That's wonderful. I haven't emptied my bathroom trashcan yet. We can just dig them back out."

"We can prove you're innocent." Brooklyn

clutched her mother's arm, looking just as enthused as Ansley.

But Ward shook his head. "No. You don't understand. It doesn't matter if I can prove it or not. Caren bought into his bluff. She showed me just how much she doesn't support me or trust me. She'd never back me up if I really needed it. I wouldn't go back to her now if she begged."

"And you shouldn't," Desi huffed. "I'm not going back either. We'll just have to start our own center. Something a million times better than Danny's Haven."

"Yeah," Tara and Jace agreed, cheering in unison.

Ward snorted. "Yeah, that would be great. Just show me the cash to start a project like that." Caren had started Danny's Haven with tons of insurance money she'd gotten after her son, Danny, had overdosed on prescription drugs.

Everyone fell silent, deliberating their newest problem. Then Ansley perked up.

"What about the money you saved back for Brooklyn?" She turned to everyone else. "He told me he'd been saving up for years. There must be enough to get a decent down payment for a loan. And being a loan officer, I know I can find enough grants and endowments to help this center get off its feet."

"But that's for Brooklyn," Ward started.

"Don't worry, Dad. It's okay." His daughter patted his arm. "I don't need it."

"But what about college. Or . . ."

"Dad, I'm a straight A student. Haven't you ever heard of scholarships? I'll be fine."

"But —"

"Seriously," she cut in, holding up a hand. "It's either I buy a super nice car with it or let you use it as a down payment to build a center to help save hundreds of teens' lives. What do you think I'm going to choose?"

Amazed, Ward sent a dazed look Ansley's way. "You have one amazing daughter, Miss Marlow."

She just grinned. "She's yours too, Mr. Gemmell."

He couldn't contain himself a moment longer. He reached out and snagged her close. A startled gasp was the only sound to exit her lips. But she melted against him soon enough and even wrapped her arms around his neck. "I really love you," he said when he pulled back just enough to gaze into her warm brown eyes.

She blushed but grinned back. "I love you, too."

Forget waiting to date her until he was

settled. He wouldn't be settled until he was her husband. She was too amazing to live without. And her daughter was too amazing to live without. Their faith, love and support of him proved it.

"Will you marry me?" he asked, pressing his forehead to hers.

Her eyes widened but soon enough she blinked and smiled. "Yes." Then she screamed out a happy yelp. "Yes!" Leaping back against him, she kissed him harder.

Clapping interrupted them. Ward lifted his face to find Desi, Jace, Tara and Brooklyn applauding as they watched.

"Don't mind us," Brooklyn said, wiping at her moist eyes as she laughed and smiled. "This is better than any happy ending I've ever seen on any movie."

Epilogue

Six Years Later

Church bells rang, announcing the noon hour. Since the wedding was supposed to start at twelve sharp, Ansley turned from the doors of the vestibule to look for the wedding coordinator. It was time to start.

When she spotted her husband wincing as he tried to straighten his bowtie, she grinned. Brooklyn had told Ward he didn't have to wear one, but he'd insisted that he wanted to look like a respectable father of the bride. He would wear the bow tie. And he obviously hated every second of it.

Strolling toward him, Ansley softly batted his fingers away. "Here. Let me." She grasped the ends of the black cloth and pulled it snug, making it neat and straight.

Ward lifted his chin to allow her better access. But with his sexy throat exposed, she couldn't resist leaning forward to kiss the warm skin along the side of his neck. Aftershave tickled her nostrils, making her hum with delight. She loved his smell.

Ward groaned and caught her shoulders. "Does this mean you like how I look in a tux, Mrs. Gemmell?"

She laughed and snuggled close, burrowing against his warm, solid chest. "This means I always like how you look."

He chuckled and hugged her tight, kissing her hair. "Ditto. That dress looks lovely on you. I hope you plan to save me a dance at the reception?"

Grinning, she kissed his throat again, just under his ear. "Count on it."

"Okay, okay. Enough of that, you two." Desi, their self-proclaimed wedding coordinator, clapped her hands as she broke them up. "We have a wedding to start. Ansley, I just sent your parents down the aisle. So it's your turn."

She motioned to the waiting usher, so Ansley squeezed Ward's hand. "Take care of our baby." And then she was off, entering the sanctuary.

Jace stood at the front of the church, next to the pastor. When he glanced back to send her a wide grin, she nodded and smiled back. Thanking the usher, Ansley took her seat at the front next to her mother.

She was glad her parents had finally come

around. But three years ago, about the same time Dr. Preston B. Jackson had been sued by a patient for malpractice and lost his medical license, they had finally approached Ansley and stopped the silent treatment they'd been giving her since she and Ward had married. Now, they were slowly becoming part of Ansley, Brooklyn, and Ward's family again.

Patting her mother's hand, Ansley turned to watch Tara, the maid of honor, carry a bouquet down the aisle to the front of the church.

Since that Sunday morning in Ward's old apartment when the six of them had created the idea for Teen Right, a new drug clinic for the city's youth, Tara and Brooklyn had grown to be best friends. Actually, she and Brooklyn, and Jace, along with Ward and Desi were the five main counselors at Teen Right. The three youngest had graduated from college last spring and were now full-time employees.

Ansley couldn't be prouder of them. To see all the work they had put into the center come to fruition was like a dream come true for all of them. She'd almost been as happy on the opening day as she was today.

When the music changed to the wedding march, everyone stood and Ansley turned to watch her husband and daughter appear in the doorway.

Her family.

Tears clogged her lashes while Brooklyn, clutching Ward's arm, gazed toward the front of the room until she caught Jace's eye.

Unable to help herself, Ansley peeked back to catch the groom's expression. Brooklyn hadn't let him see her wedding dress and now that he was laying eyes on it, or more aptly on the bride inside it, he looked dazed speechless.

So happy that her child had found a love like what she'd been able to find with Ward, Ansley fumbled with her clutch purse to release the snap and yank out a tissue. But her mother reached out, handing her one first.

Murmuring her gratitude, Ansley wiped her eyes and heaved in a breath when she caught Ward watching her as he passed. With a wink, he escorted Brooklyn to Jace and gave their daughter away.

ABOUT THE AUTHOR

The youngest of eight children, **Linda Kage** grew up on a dairy farm in the Midwest. She now lives in Kansas with her husband, daughter and nine cuckoo clocks. Linda is a member of Romance Writers of America and its local chapter, Midwest Romance Writers.

LindaKage.com